I0762289

The events in this story are drawn directly from fact.

First Printing, 2023

ISBN (print edition): 9780645378443
ISBN (eBook): 9780645378450

Front Cover: Chinese on the road to the Palmer. The Australasian Sketcher, 12/06/1875. Courtesy: State Library Victoria. 1655614; b50050.
Back Cover: "Chinese camp, Beechworth", by Thomas Hannay (c. 1859) Courtesy: State Library Victoria. 3250483; is009880.

ALSO AVAILABLE FROM THIS SERIES

Ah Nam
Joe Byrne and the Cow from El Dorado

COMING SOON

Ned Kelly and the Two Kings
The Temptations of Joe Byrne
The Horrors at Sebastopol

AN OUTLAW'S JOURNAL

AN OUTLAW'S JOURNAL

Blood and Bamboo

GEORGINA STONES

Aidan Phelan

Australian Bushranging

Contents

A MYSTERIOUS DEATH

Dedicated to

Joseph Byrne

Aaron Sherritt

Ellen Byron

As well as the people of Beechworth, Sebastopol and Greta who feature throughout this book.

And to my darling husband, Aidan Phelan.

A Note from the Author

To my dear reader, what you are about to consume is a dramatised narrative based on my historical research. I believe that this is a way to make the past more vivid and relatable for those of us that were not there in a way "straight" non-fiction cannot. It is also a way for me to contextualise the broader research that I have done in a way that shows how it relates to the history without being dry or distracting the readers from the core of the story. All too often in traditional history books the author will side-track the reader with footnotes, sidenotes and appendices, and we end up losing our place in the story. Now everything will seamlessly blend together for your enjoyment as much as your education. But for those hoping for a "facts and figures" approach to history, never fear — following the narrative you will find a summary of my research, how it relates to what you will have just read, and even some of the source material transcribed for you to read. It may have taken months — years, in fact — for me to find and compile this information, but for you it is all in this one convenient location. You will see that what I have written is no mere fantasy but rather an informed interpretation of everything I have discovered to date about Joe Byrne, those who were a part of his life, the places and times he lived in, and the reality of what happens to a young man faced with the many challenges, temptations and disadvantages he faced during his brief time on this earth.

Without further ado, I invite you to enjoy your journey into the past as you delve into the following pages. I know that I have enjoyed writing them for you.

— Georgina Stones.

Prologue

Elly lies curled against my chest, the pair of us seeking what warmth we can from the small fire that burns in the stone hearth. The hut we are sheltering in is not my own, but one belonging to Ned Kennedy although he has long deserted it.

I have brought Elly up here after spending the day with Aaron Sherritt branding stolen fillies in the yard outside. The blue one he had entrusted me with was rather lively and did not hesitate in exacting revenge for the red-hot brand that was levelled at her shoulder. She knocked the bark clean from my shin and left a bloodied gash. Aaron did not give me much pity, preferring instead to joke that it was my receipt of sale, but Elly showed me plenty. She tenderly cleaned the wound with iodine, just as she had done after my scuffle with Ah Nam and Robert Woods all those years ago. The damn stuff stung like the cut of a cane but I was too lost in the view of her to give it much care.

Elly is to be married soon, to a man named Byron, a 29-year-old herdsman from Chiltern, eleven years her senior. Her father has recently found me unsuitable; it seems being a drunkard is preferable to lifting the odd calf or filly. I tried to challenge his stance, but his mind was set like stone. I wish I had enough coin to take her away from here so that we may live a life of our choosing, but fencing Aaron's selection does not pay well.

"My Elly," I murmur, stroking my fingers through her hair, "you really are the most beautiful woman in all the Woolshed."

She narrows her eyes.

"Only the Woolshed?"

"I'm not well travelled," I respond with a wink.

She strokes a hand across my face, her finger tracing the hairs of my moustache, tickling my top lip.

"I will miss this, Joe," she whispers, "nothing will ever be the same for us."

"I know, Elly. I know."

I turn my face away as tears blur my vision and focus on the assortment of moths that flutter above me. My heart aches at the thought of her being stolen from me, left to become Byron's wife and the mother of his children. For her sake, I have tried my best to hide my anger and hurt but I cannot deny that I have wished to lay the bugger out.

Shifting my weight on the bunk I look down at her, her face cast in shadow. I kiss the curve of her jaw and allow my hand to cup the roundness of her breast, squeezing it gently. Elly used to complain about the roughness of my hands, calloused from months of digging fence posts and felling trees on Aaron's selection, but her protests have since fallen silent. I pull her close and breathe in her scent, pushing back thoughts of having to let her go. I want to savour the feel and taste of her, with no way of knowing when we will next be together all I have is the present.

I

The visions of Ellen Salisbury on their last night together dissipates from Joe's mind as he is brought back to the present by the sharp nudging elbow of Aaron Sherritt.

"Are you bloody coming with me to Sheepstation or not?" He snaps abruptly.

Joe looks at his mate confused, feeling as if he has joined mid-conversation.

"Hmm?"

Aaron rolls his eyes and flicks at the brim of Joe's porkpie hat.

"You've not heard a word I've said, have you?"

"I was thinking about Ellen," he replies, looking over his shoulder at the granite fortress that is Beechworth Gaol, surprised at the distance he has travelled while his mind has been elsewhere.

"You need to forget her," Aaron remarks casually. "Isn't she supposed to be getting married to that herdsman from Chiltern?"

Joe stops walking and glares at Aaron.

"I wouldn't *need* to forget her if you weren't forever scheming to get us lagged."

Aaron scoffs at the accusation.

"We've had a taste of Her Majesty's hospitality," he says with a show of bravado. "We know what to expect now. It could have been worse, Joe," Aaron shrugs.

Joe shakes his head in disbelief.

"Worse? Because we weren't dangling from the gallows?"

"There, you said it yourself, could have been worse."

Joe steps closer to Aaron and takes a fistful of his lapel.

"You'll not get me in there again, Sherritt, I bloody swear it."

"Going to walk the straight and narrow, are you? Find respectable employment?" Aaron asks, his voiced laced in spite.

Joe prods him firmly in the shoulder.

"I will if it keeps me out of there. Borrowing horses and lifting the odd filly and calf was a lark when we weren't getting caught. But how many times do you have to be locked away before you realise the game is up?"

"They can't lag you if you're smart, Joe. We were foolish last time."

"No, *you* were foolish!" Joe asserts, his voice raised louder than intended, causing onlookers to stare at the two young men. Joe feels embarrassed. His cropped hair and ill-fitting clothes giving away his previous existence as plainly as if he was still dressed in the grey woollen prison garb.

Joe turns away from his mate and doubles back.

"Oi, where are you going?" Aaron calls from behind him.

"Home," he answers over his shoulder.

II

Despite half a year having passed since Joe was last in the Woolshed Valley, it appeared as if no time had passed at all. The land still bearing a yellow colouring after the prolonged drought that has gripped the region during the winter months of 1876, with sluicing in Reedy Creek only having properly resumed during Joe's final months in prison, after miners were left to abandon their claims and watch helplessly as the creek level dropped.

Arriving at Sebastopol, Joe's eyes drift to a pair of wedge-tailed eagles that fly above him, circling the steep gullies of pine and granite that enclose the flat, in search of prey.

Joe walks through the Chinese camp, the lively atmosphere a far cry from the confines of a lonely gaol cell. Noticing Joe, Ah Lim, a store-keeper who had employed Joe after the death of his father Paddy six years previously, emerges from his shop.

"Néih hóu, Ah Joe! Good see you out of gaol!" He calls from under the bark awning. "No good place for man like you."

Stepping aside for an elderly Chinese market gardener shouldering a yoke laden with spring vegetables, Joe lowers his head in greeting.

"Néih hóu, Ah Lim. I will do my best to stay out of trouble."

Ah Lim laughs at the remark and unfurls the fabric banner that has been wound around the veranda post by the breeze.

"I believe when my eyes see it, Ah Joe."

Continuing down the well-worn track of the camp's main thoroughfare, Joe passes the store of Yee Fang. The brutal scenes of the torture of Ah Suey, wantonly fill his mind. They take him back to the spot as a wide-eyed 15-year-old, watching with the throng of shocked onlookers as the defenceless miner was humiliated and ill-treated by Ye On and Hung Young, who had been in Yee Fang's employ. The trauma had resulted in many sleepless nights, no matter how many times he had thumped at his temples in an attempt to relieve his mind of Ah Suey's cries.

Focusing his attention ahead of him, Joe notices John Harvey mounting his bay mare in front of Ah Shoo's restaurant.

"Hullo, mate," acknowledges John, tightening the reins. He looks curiously at Joe's cropped hair.

Joe feels his cheeks prickling under John's judgement.

"Hullo, Mr. Harvey," he answers briefly, not wishing to attract any more attention.

Walking across the footbridge over Reedy Creek, Joe passes the Batchelor homestead and lowers his head, hoping no one is home to see his return from gaol. His failure to return Jane Batchelor's knives and steel after the incident with the cow had been noted, the petty old biddy had even brought it up as evidence at the trial. The Batchelors was also where Ellen had been employed as a domestic servant, with Joe spending many late afternoons waiting for her to finish her shift there. These memories tugging at his heart, he picks up his pace.

***

As Joe nears his mother's selection, he sees the hut belonging to Ah

On and his three mates, isolated from the other Chinese huts that sit clustered together.

Ah On is busy working in the market garden as Joe passes, he pauses tilling and looks up at Joe, neither saying a word, before he turns his attention back to the soil.

Since his wild brawl with Ah Fook in 1874, in which he had crippled the miner with blows from a bamboo pole, the other Chinese had ostracised Ah On. This had left Ah Fook unable to work and he could only crawl around the camp. The mistrust had only grown since Ah Fook's body had been found lying in a patch of scrub, mutilated and castrated. While there was no evidence these brutal acts had been carried out by Ah On's hand, the rumours had spread. A ruling of suicide had been passed, but even Joe's foe Mounted-Constable Mullane had his suspicions.

Joe's disliking of the man had started over the use of the dam that was close to Ah On's hut. Despite it being open to use, Ah On had taken ownership of the water. On hot summer days, Joe would look longingly at the cool water but, no matter how many attempts he made, Ah On would always spy him before he could dip a toe in.

On a particularly hot day, in an act of spite, Joe had thrown rocks at the man's hut, taunting him and the two other men then bolting when they had threatened him with bamboos.

***

Arriving at his mother's house, Joe glances at the front paddock where the small heard of milking cows stand beneath the shade of a gum tree, their rib and hip bones jutting beneath dirty hides.

He raps his knuckles against the door and steels himself for the welcome he knows he will receive.

The bolt is drawn and his mother Margaret opens the door ajar, her eyes widening on the gaol hardened figure of her eldest son.

"Joe?"

He offers her a smile.

"I thought I'd save Patsy the embarrassment of coming to meet me outside the gaol gate."

Margaret opens the door, her bare forearms covered in a dusting of flour. She nods and goes back to the kitchen. Joe follows her.

Mother and son stand awkwardly in the small kitchen of the hut, neither knowing how to react. Joe clears his throat.

"I'm sorry for what I put you through, Ma. That was never my intention."

With an air of indifference, Margaret moves back to the table and resumes kneading the piece of dough.

"By the state yer in, ye will be needing some new clothes," she remarks, leaving Joe's apology to hang, unanswered, in the air.

Joe tugs at the sleeve of his jacket, the ill-fitting material biting at his wrist.

"They had me working pretty hard," he offers, memories of breaking granite with a sledgehammer surfacing in his mind, "Aaron's clothes are as badly fitting as mine."

"Where is Sherritt?" Margaret asks, shaping the dough.

"Back at Sheepstation Creek. I'll be staying away from him for a while."

"Oh?" Margaret, responds. She goes to quiz Joe further, but the call of Paddy's voice from outside halts her inquisitiveness.

"I've patched the fence, Ma," he announces.

Joe walks towards the window and peers through the smudgy pane at his younger brother.

"Joe!" Paddy exclaims, noticing the familiar face.

Within moments, Paddy is inside, his arms outstretched. The brothers embrace.

"Hullo, Patsy, you've been busy I see?"

Paddy nods.

"Been helping Ma as best as I can while home. Picked up some work across the border."

Even though he knows it is not his brother's intention, Joe feels the words are directed at his own failures.

"That's grand," he says, uncomfortably.

Paddy removes his hat, dropping it on the table, the unthinking action earning a disapproving glance from his mother as she marks a cross in the dough and pokes each corner with a knife to release the fairies. Placing the dough into a cast iron pot, Margaret hangs the pot over the fire and wipes her floured hands across her apron with a sigh.

"I'm making some tea," she declares, checking on the kettle.

"Yes please, Ma," says Joe.

"I bet you're looking forward to some decent grub after the stuff you've been fed in gaol?" Paddy asks, taking a spot along the bench of the dining table. He looks at Joe expectantly.

"Aye. You never want to find yourself behind that wall, Patsy," Joe answers bluntly, joining him at the table without further word. Paddy looks disappointed by Joe's response.

"What was it like?" Paddy asks, after a pause.

"Aaron would be the one to tell you, he seems to have a different memory of it all than I do."

"Where is Aaron?"

"Gone home," Joe answers, watching as his mother drops tea leaves into their teapot and fills it with boiling water.

Paddy raises an eyebrow and looks on Joe with a quizzical expression. But is given no further response from Joe.

"Denny and Maggie will be pleased to see you when they're home from school," he announces.

"Aye. I look forward to seeing them too."

III

The day after his release is the anniversary of his father's death. His uncle Michael Byrne calls in to see the family, as he does every year on the 7th of November to see if there is anything he can do to aid the family. He is a man in his forties who closely resembles his deceased brother, but with a more square, hardened visage.

After greeting the family and placing a muslin parcel on the table, his grey eyes come to rest on Joe.

"What's this?" He asks, gesturing to Joe's cropped hair.

Joe does not have the nerve to answer. Margaret chides his silence with a scowl.

"Joseph has just come out of Beechworth Gaol," she says coldly, "he was in there for six months would yer believe."

Joe bows his head in shame.

"Boy!" Michael reprimands, "Look up at me. What's this about? What got ye inside?"

"I butchered a cow with my mate," Joe replies, his voice low.

"Speak up, boy."

"It was the school cow, over at El Dorado. We butchered it and got six months each with hard labour."

Michael shakes his head as Margaret gestures with the teapot.

"Yer a damn fool, Joseph. Yer Da has been gone for six years; yer meant to be the man of the house. The provider. Not rotting in a gaol cell. What would yer father think? He'd have been ashamed after all we done to shake off the convict stain."

Joe's hold on his gaze wavers.

"I know."

"Well, if ye know, make sure ye never get within those walls again. If it's meat ye need, me and yer uncle John are here to help. Yer no good to yer mother or brothers and sisters in gaol. Remember, boy, it's English rules whether us Irish like it or not. They'll crush yer soon as look at yer, so ye've gotta be smart."

Joe nods.

"I believe there was an offer of tea," Michael says, his expression softening.

***

It has been a week since Joe walked out of the wooden gates of Beechworth Gaol as a free man and he had not seen Aaron since then. Even though he has wondered how he was getting on with his selection and if he required help felling trees and patching fences, he had stayed away. He refuses to allow himself to be pulled back into Aaron's thoughtless schemes that would inevitably land him back behind the dock.

Standing at the washing line, Joe plays a tune on the concertina. His sister Kate pegs damp washing along the line, which is kept taut by two branches dug into the ground.

"Have you seen Ellen, Kate?" Joe asks meekly.

Kate picks up an undershirt from the wicker basket and shakes out the creases before pegging it to the line.

"She's upset that you haven't been to see her, Joe. She knows you're out of prison."

"How can I visit her? She's a married woman now. I can't be seen hanging around."

"She thinks you don't want to see her."

"I don't want to see her? How can she think that? I'm staying away because it's how it has to be. For her sake."

Kate reaches for another item of clothing and frowns at her brother.

"Ellen doesn't see it that way and nor do I, Joe. You need to ride over and see her, instead of feeling sorry for yourself."

Joe's thoughts mull over Kate's suggestion, his head and heart pulling him in different directions.

"Besides, it's not like you to be worried about doing the wrong thing," Kate continues, cheekily.

"I do when it involves Ellen."

The burden playing on his mind causing him to mindlessly squeeze the concertina, startling Kate's bay filly who grazes beside the fence. The startled horse snorts and trots toward the middle of the yard, halting to look at Joe with her ears pricked.

"At least have a think about it, for Ellen's sake, Joe," Kate says, picking up the empty basket.

***

For the past few days, Joe has mulled over Kate's words. He has wrestled with the idea that he is feeling sorry for himself and has tried to convince himself that it is not so. In reality, he would love nothing more than to send Byron to kingdom come and take Ellen away to live fearless, free and bold like outlaws, but he knows it cannot be. *She is married to Byron, sharing his bed and raising his children.* Joe's jaw clenches. He paces backwards and forwards along the length of veranda, his thoughts a jumbled mess.

After several anxious minutes, there is a sharp tap on the window.

"Stop walking a track in the dirt like a lost sheep and make yerself useful, Joseph!" His mother demands, glaring at him through the glass.

Joe makes a flippant gesture with his hand and reaches for the axe that rests against the side of the house, hoping the act of chopping firewood will work to clear his mind and keep his mother's nagging at bay.

Lining up the log, Joe splits it, the dull thud of the axe echoing around the flat as he works. *Perhaps if I had worked harder Ellen would still be mine? If I had told Aaron and his scheming mind to go to hell, I would have been allowed a few extra months with Ellen, before she had become Byron's wife. But what hope do I have now? She is married. Mrs Byron of the Black Dog Creek.* Joe feels his anger rise. Training his mind on the task before him, he strikes the blade into the wood with an impassioned cry.

***

With Kate having finally convinced Joe to go and see Ellen, he rides toward Lancashire Gap, following the course of Black Dog Creek that snakes around the township of Chiltern.

He arrives at a hut with a bark exterior secured by poles of Stringybark and small garden bed of daisies, as Kate had described to him. Joe halts Music and dismounts, his gaze settling wistfully on a lonely sheep that grazes in a poorly fenced front paddock. He had gifted the animal to Ellen as a lamb, after finding it shivering in the gully, next to the body of its mother. Being weak with cold and hunger, the animal was easy to catch and bundle beneath his coat. Snow, she had called her.

Leading Music to the hitching rail, he tethers her and takes an armful of hay from the stack that is positioned next to the hut and places it on the ground for her to pick at.

Walking toward the hut, a sheep dog that has been lazing in the sun outside its kennel begins to bark at the unfamiliar figure. Joe ignores its bluff and knocks at the door.

"Who is it?" Ellen asks from inside.

Joe makes a familiar bird call.

The bolt is drawn with a rattle and the door opened. Ellen peers out and focuses on Joe with tired eyes, the skin around them darkened by lack of sleep. Her thin appearance taking him aback as she steps out from the shadows of the hut.

"Joe?" A slight gasp escaping her lips, "I wasn't expecting to see you."

"Is *he* about?" Joe asks, his voice a low whisper.

Ellen shakes her head.

"No. Martin is down at the Chiltern Common. He is probably lying on his back drunk, but that is where he is."

"Can I come in," Joe asks cautiously.

Ellen's blue eyes flick over the young man in front of her; his auburn hair still cropped short from his time in prison and the muscles of his chest and upper arms more defined after his time breaking rock. She beckons him inside.

Stepping into the hut, Joe scans the interior; the front room is sparsely furnished, with the walls lined with hessian bags. Sitting over the hearth is a small framed *carte de visite* of the couple, taken to commemorate their marriage. Joe scowls at the portrait and turns away from it, his eyes resting on a crib in the corner of the room. His heart sinking like lead in his chest.

Joe looks down at the infant, a rush of tangled emotion he has not felt before pulses through him. *Jealously? Heartbreak? Grief? Anger?* Joe is not certain. He has never thought much about babies and families, always preferring to take each day as it comes. A 'drifter' Ellen's father had called him, after the Norfolk native had decided Joe was no longer suitable for his daughter. But seeing what he could have had with Ellen, Joe suddenly yearns for nothing more.

Ellen moves toward the cot, smoothing the woollen blanket that is tucked beneath the baby's chin.

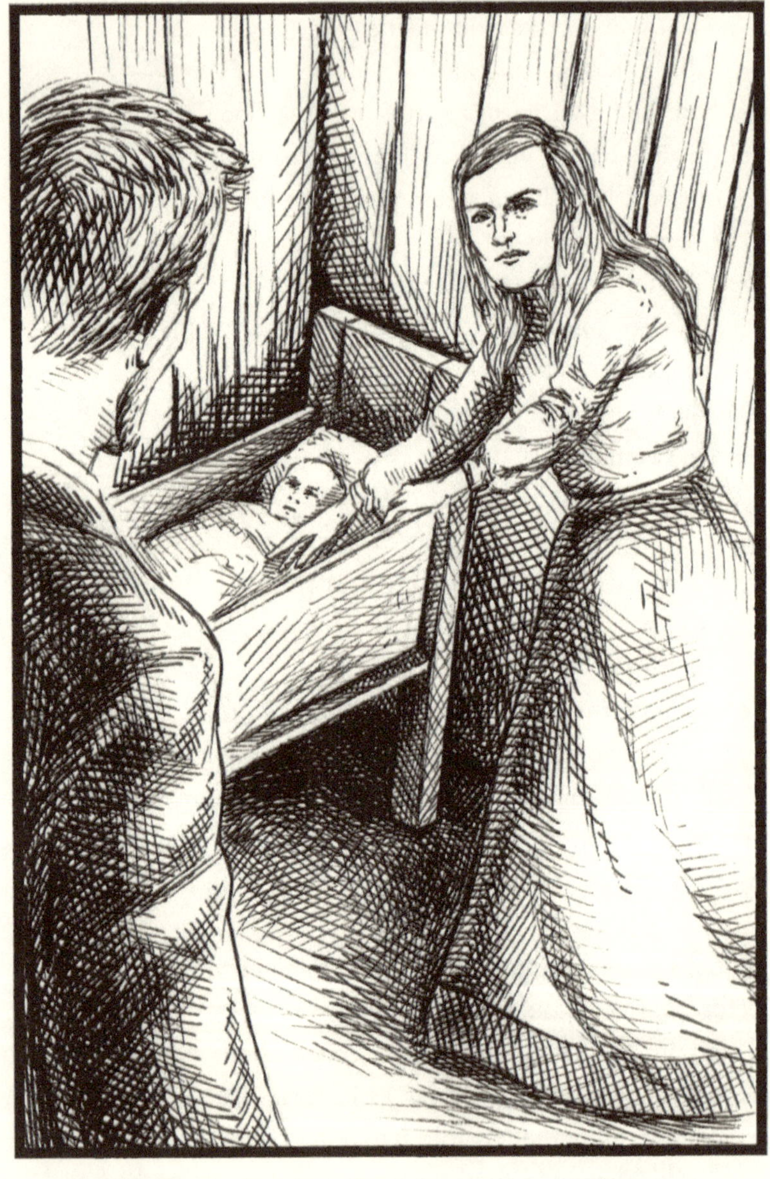

"James Martin, he has called him. I gave birth in October. Elizabeth helped with the delivery."

"October?" Joe repeats, confused, "But you only married Byron in July?"

Ellen glances up at Joe with a pained expression.

"I was five months pregnant when I married Martin, Joe."

Their eyes lock as the words hang, heavy, in the air, neither wishing to address them.

Wordlessly, she moves towards the dining table and touches the teapot to see if it is warm.

"I thought you had forgotten about me. When Kate told me you were out of gaol, I couldn't understand why you hadn't come to me."

"I wanted to Elly," Joe says, sitting at the table, "but I didn't think I'd be welcome. Not with you married."

Ellen pours Joe a cup of the steaming tawny coloured tea and passes it to him.

"I've been so alone. My only visitors have been your sister and Elizabeth. I needed you, Joe, but you never came."

Joe reaches for her hand, but she pulls it away.

"It has been awful Joe," she continues, 'Lord Byron' he is calling himself now. I've never known embarrassment like it. He has so many enemies, owing to his gambling debts, and I have no way of knowing when another attempt will be made at burning down the house. If it wasn't for me and my brothers, this house would never have been built. He was never sober enough to work."

Joe holds his head in his hands, finally realising what Ellen has been through. When she needed him the most, he was too busy wallowing in self-pity.

"Didn't you say yourself that nothing would change between us, no matter what Martin or my father said."

"Yes," Joe replies, his voice strained, "but you weren't married then and living 24 miles away. If Byron catches me, he'll have me tied to that fence out there and flogged."

"That wasn't my decision Joe," she says, slamming the pannikin down on the table. "I couldn't have gone to you, but you could have come to me at any time. Did you even ask how I was?"

"Of course I did, but most men don't take kindly to other men hanging around their wives."

"Martin will need to be sober enough to notice," Ellen snaps resentfully. "I am willing to keep up the front for the sake of my baby, but he will never truly have my heart. Not the way you do."

Joe holds her hands in his.

"I have missed you terribly, Elly. When Kate told me you thought I didn't want to see you, it damn near broke my heart. How could you think a thing like that?"

"I worried about you every day while you were in prison. Thank goodness for Kate, she is the only person I could confide in. I am sure I would have gone mad with the worrying otherwise," Ellen replies. "But I never heard from you, what was I supposed to think?"

Joe squeezes her hand reassuringly.

"I know it can never be like it was, but I will do my best. Byron hasn't stolen you yet."

IV

The December heat clings against Joe as he works on repairing the damaged stretch of fencing of one of the paddocks of his mother's selection after a bullock had pushed through it, looking for feed.

Joe and his younger brother Denny had spent the morning herding the beasts back into the paddock after they had escaped, which had proven difficult, with the animals concerning themselves more with the pursuit of greener pastures, than going back into the yard.

Joe had tried his best to remain calm and be patient with Denny, while he hunted them; the act of herding cattle and horses seeming to always get him on edge. The unpredictable nature of the animals bringing with it its own challenges, with one mistake capable of undoing hours of work. Joe had asked his 12-year-old sister Mary to come and help, but she had outright refused. Still harbouring resentment at how she had been treated when he had last requested her help. On that occasion, Joe had asked her to stand in a gap of Ned Kennedy's yard and act as a deterrent, should one of the young horses he and Aaron had yarded tried their luck. Having managed to direct them into the yard, Joe was determined to put a halter on the black colt. The young animal had trotted skittishly around the yard, looking desperately for a place of escape, with Joe ordering his sister to stand firm when he had noticed her faltering. The colt took his chance, and rushed at Mary, causing her to jump out of the way for fear of being knocked over. Joe had been beside himself and had run up to his sister, striking her across the face with the halter for the trouble she had caused him.

Shaking his head, ashamed at how he had hurt the child, Joe gives the patched fence a rattle to test its strength. Hoping it will be strong enough to hold the bullocks in. He removes his hat and scratches a hand through his hair, the sweat causing his scalp to itch, and looks across at the cooling water of the dam. *Just a quick drink, then back to work*, he thinks. He picks up the water bucket and heads to the dam.

At the dam Joe kneels and skims the bucket over the top of the water to top it up. He cups some in his hand and slurps at it. Hearing a banging behind him, he turns to see Ah On at the window of his hut bashing at the window frame.

"No, no, no!" The miner yells. "Mine! Mine!"

Joe replies by jabbing two fingers in the air at Ah On.

Turning his back on the dam, he returns to the farm, where he sees his mother waiting for him.

"Where were ye?" Margaret asks abruptly.

Joe lifts the bucket and she looks across at the patched fence, swatting a collection of flies that buzz around her face. She takes the bucket and turns to take it inside without a word.

Margaret's indifference to him since his release from prison has been jabbing at Joe like an iron poker. He knows he has never been a model son and he has done everything he could think of, but now it feels like she is actively trying to drive him away.

He follows his mother into the house. "I don't know what it is you want from me, Ma," he declares, standing in the doorway.

Margaret places the wooden bucket on the table with a thud, causing the water to lap at the sides.

"I don't want *anything* from ye, Joseph," she responds, brushing back auburn wisps that fall about her face.

"Are you unhappy with me, then?"

Margaret places her hands on her hips with a sigh.

"What is this about?"

Joe clears his throat.

"I feel like you don't want me here?"

"What do ye want me to say? Should I be *proud* that ye were locked up in prison for six months, while we were left struggling to get by? There was no rain for months, Joseph. No grass for the cows and nothing for me to churn. We were left surviving off Catherine's wage and whatever Patrick brought in."

"How am I to blame for the weather?" He retorts. "I'm always doing my best to help."

"How many chances do you want me to give ye, Joseph? Yer 20 years old. Most men have their own selection at that age. Heavens, even Sherritt has managed that!"

"Sherritt only has that selection because his father helped pay for it and he has *me* to help clear and fence it."

"I have six other children who need my help, Joseph, I cannot keep worrying myself on yer account. Not anymore."

Joe remains silent, the fight no longer in him.

"Right. I'll be off then."

***

With nowhere else to go, Joe heads to the one place he knows he is welcome - Sheepstation Creek. He has tried to make a go of it, to show his mother he can put his family first and be the man of the house, but what good is it if it is not welcome?

Coming to the dense bush that flanks Stoney Creek, Joe spurs Music into a canter and mutters under his breath. *I am tired of trying, tired of apologising, tired of just being seen as a pair of hands to do chores and never being good enough at that.*

***

Aaron is ringbarking trees when Joe arrives at his selection, his shirt sleeves rolled up past his sunburnt forearms, a layer of sweat glistening across his forehead. Noticing Joe walking towards him, Aaron raises an arm and wedges the axe blade into the trunk.

"I knew you couldn't stay away," he says with a smirk.

Joe ignores him and sits on a stump, his gaze focused on the rocky outcrop that borders the creek

"I tried my best, but it still wasn't good enough."

Aaron tears at a piece of loose bark that hangs from the tree.

"What happened?"

"Ma," Joe says, shielding his eyes from the sun as he looks up at his mate, "I think she even blames me for the bloody drought."

Aaron raises an eyebrow and untucks his shirt from his moleskins, flapping the material to allow the breeze to cool his skin.

"Well, that's a new one. She's a tough old biddy."

"I'm done trying. Nothing I do will ever be good enough."

"And how's my darlin' Katie?" Aaron asks, pulling a flask from his pocket to swig.

"All the better for being away from you," Joe replies sarcastically, gesturing for the flask, "she convinced me to visit Ellen."

"How'd that go?"

Joe sniffs at the contents of the flask, the fumes from the alcohol burning his eyes. He takes a swig, wincing at the roughness of the whiskey.

"She's got a baby," Joe croaks, tossing the flask back to Aaron. "Where the hell did you get this stuff?"

"From Evan's in the Woolshed. The cheapest I could find."

"Aye, tastes like it."

Aaron shoves it back into his pocket.

"Where do things stand between you and Ellen? I doubt Byron would be too pleased to know you're hanging around his wife."

"Who said he knew I was there?" Joe states, rising from the stump, "Besides, what he doesn't know can't hurt him. He should consider himself lucky he didn't have a decent horse; I'd have brought it home."

Aaron throws his head back and laughs at his mate's bluster.

"Ride his horse, ride his wife," he declares with a knowing wink.

"Aye, something like that. Got anything better to drink?"

"Help me with these last few trees and we'll head to the Vine. There's a new barmaid working there, she looks alright," Aaron says with a sly grin.

"Alright," Joe replies, taking out his pipe.

***

The substantial brick building with its shingled roof that is the Vine Hotel sits along Sydney Road in Beechworth, its orchard of fruit trees backing on to the town's cemetery, where Joe's father Paddy and infant brother John lie.

Walking along the veranda, an old man dressed in a miner's smock and dirt crusted boots sniggers at the shaven pair.

"Fresh out of Beechworth dungeons, eh?" He slurs through a large greasy beard.

Aaron replies with an upturned gesture of his fingers, while Joe ignores the man and lowers his hat. His namesake and grandfather, Joseph Byrne, a rebel from County Carlow, had experienced the ostracism first hand that was the convict stain, after being transported for life to the colony of New South Wales for 'unlawful oaths.' Joe's experience since his release from gaol has given him a taste of what his forebears endured.

Joe and Aaron take a spot at the bar, jostling for space between the assortment of drinkers.

Joe's eyes fall on Mrs. Vandenburg's daughter and a young woman with mousey-brown ringlets tucked beneath a cloth cap, as the two women bustle about behind the bar, trying their best to keep up with the afternoon influx of drinkers.

Noticing Joe and Aaron at the bar, the woman smiles, holding their attention.

"Good afternoon gentleman, what can I be serving you both?" She asks, her Cornish accent rising over the loud hum of chatter.

"Two nobblers of gin, please," Aaron asserts, sliding the appropriate coin across the bar. The young woman tucks the money into a pocket of her apron.

Joe watches while she takes a square bottle of gin from the shelf and pours an equal amount of the spirit into each glass.

Aaron leans on his elbows and offers her a cheeky smile.

"New in town, eh?"

"I am," she replies, sliding the nobblers across the bar, the motion causing the fabric of her sleeve to rise and Joe notices a purple burn mark on her wrist. Aware of Joe's gaze on it, she tugs at the fabric self-consciously.

"And what can I call you?" Aaron asks, the glass raised to his lips.

"Well, *you* can call me miss," she responds with a glare.

Taken aback by her touchiness, Aaron falters and nods towards Joe.

"Ah...my mate Joe here wants to know."

Joe feels his cheeks redden at being put on the spot.

"*He* can call me Maggie," she answers, gesturing towards Joe, before turning her attention to a man with an empty glass.

Joe jabs Aaron in the ribs with his elbow.

"A picture, isn't she? '*Maggie*'," Aaron muses sarcastically, attempting to mimic the Cornish accent.

Joe rolls his eye at his mate and swigs his gin.

V

The coming of Christmas has brought Joe back to his mother's selection. Not being particularly religious or constrained by the Catholic doctrine, he found the festivities more enjoyable at the Sherritts', such as their custom of a Christmas tree, influenced by Queen Victoria. However, instead of a fir tree, it was a branch of Red Box positioned in a wooden bucket and kept upright by rocks. This, the Sherritt girls would decorate with ribbon. Joe knew he would never hear the end of it if he spent the day of Christ's birth anywhere but in Sebastopol. *Perhaps I could bring some of their festivities into our house.*

Finding Margaret and Kate standing outside the larder, plucking the feathers from the Christmas turkey, Joe decides to broach the subject.

"I was thinking I'd cut a branch of the tree over there and bring it inside for little Elly and Maggie to decorate."

Margaret sighs and pauses her work.

"Whatever for, Joseph?"

"A Christmas tree, Ma. To decorate," he explains.

"A Christmas tree?" Where have ye got that idea from?" She asks snappishly.

"From the Sherritts. They have one every year and I thought it might bring some merriment."

"Well, ye thought wrong. We are Catholics, Joseph, not Protestants. I will not bring their heathen traditions into my home."

Taken aback by her refusal, Joe looks toward Kate for help.

"It could be alright, Ma," his sister says with a smile, placing a hand on Margaret's shoulder. "The girls would love it."

Margaret shakes her head and slaps Kate's hand away.

"It is bad enough a Protestant is courting my daughter. I am not having any of their ways in my house, do ye hear?"

"It's only a bit of branch," Joe continues.

"Is it?" Margaret retorts, "Well if it matters so much to ye, go and spend Christmas with the Sherritts."

***

As if she had been expecting his arrival, Joe is beckoned into the front room of the Sherritt home by Aaron's mother Anne. Any other family may have been offended at the sudden arrival of an unexpected guest to their Christmas table, but the Sherritts have grown accustomed to Joe's unannounced visits.

Stepping into the room, Joe is greeted by the family who sit gathered around the dining table, their Christmas dinner spread before them.

At the sight of his mate, Aaron raises an eyebrow.

"Get yourself in trouble *again*?"

Aaron's mother shoots her son a look of disapproval as she gestures for Joe's porkpie hat and jacket.

"Aaron," she rebukes, "that is none of yer business. Come Joseph," she continues warmly, "we have plenty to go around."

"Thank you, Mrs. Sherritt," Joe responds, feeling a tinge of embarrassment at having interrupted the family midmeal, but is grateful for the offer.

From his position at the head of the table, John Sherritt takes a mouthful of Port Wine and flicks a hand towards his children.

"Make the boy room."

The clanking of cutlery and crockery sound as the Sherritts shift their places at the table, allowing room for Joe beside Aaron.

"Fetch us a glass would ye Elizabeth," John asks, holding the bottle aloft.

Bessie rises from the table and collects one from the shelf, handing it to her father before aiding her mother in preparing Joe a plate of food.

John pours the dark coloured wine into the glass and passes it to Joe.

"Merry Christmas, son."

"Thank you, Mr. Sherritt," Joe replies, lifting the glass to his lips. He takes a sip, the sweetness of the wine causing him to purse his lips.

Beside him, Aaron stabs his fork into a piece of potato.

"What happened?"

"I suggested a Christmas tree."

Aaron tuts sarcastically while Bessie places a plate of roast turkey and vegetables on the table in front of him.

"For you, Joe."

"Thank you, Bessie," he acknowledges, taking up a knife and fork.

She sits down across from him, her hazel eyes holding his gaze.

The atmosphere around the table is much more relaxed than he is used to at home. In their company he does not feel he is judged or that he is forever in the wrong. Rather, he can enjoy himself.

***

After enjoying a helping of cherry pudding, Joe sits at the table, playing a game of euchre with Aaron, Jack, and Willie, while the women bustle about cleaning up after dinner.

Once she has finished the wiping up, Bessie disappears into a bedroom and returns with a brown paper parcel tied with twine. Shyly, she passes it to Joe.

"This is from me."

"Oh," Joe replies, surprised, "you didn't need to do that."

Peeling the paper away, Joe's eyes fall on a white handkerchief, embroidered with red and yellow flowers, and a copy of *Oliver Twist*.

"I embroidered the handkerchief myself and James Ingram in town said you would appreciate the book."

"I only got socks," Aaron says with a wink, issuing a glare from his sister.

He had long teased Joe about the feelings she had for him.

"I hope you haven't read it," she says.

"No, I haven't Bessie," Joe lies politely. "Thank you."

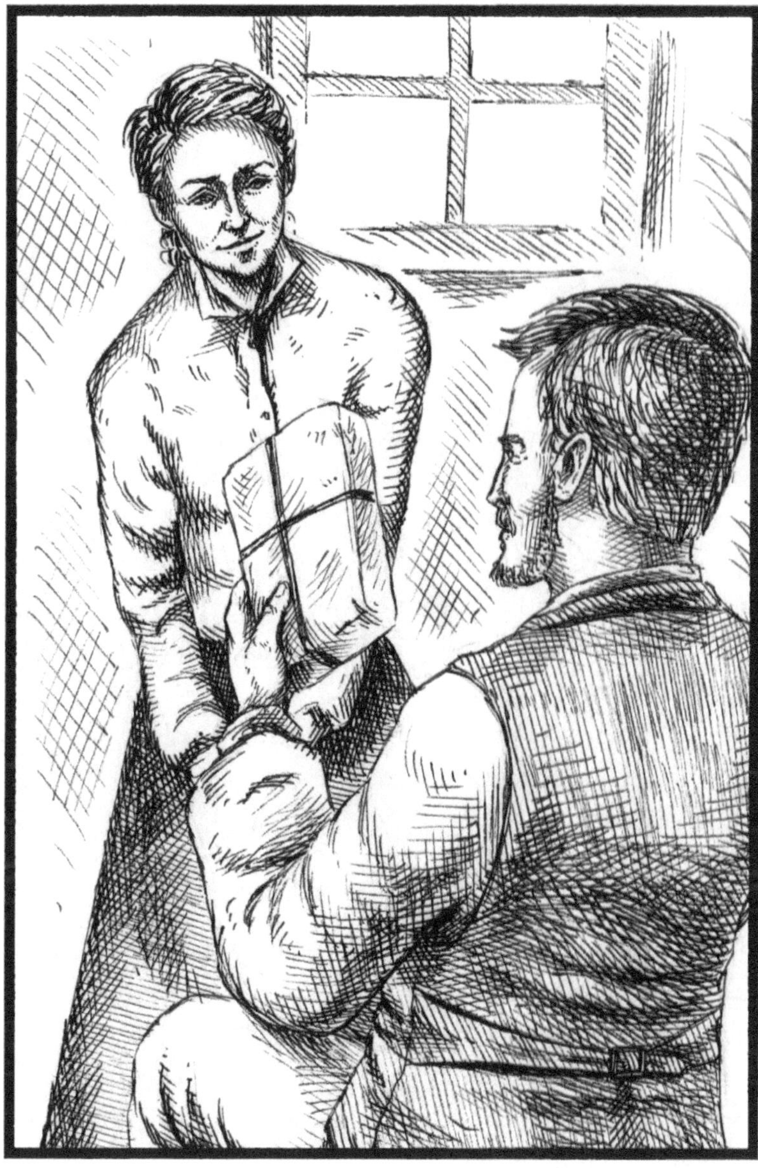

VI

Having sent word to Ellen via Kate, to meet him at Ned Kennedy's hut, Joe waits patiently for her arrival. The pair had found it difficult to reunite at their rendezvous place, with Martin Byron spending much of the time after Christmas at home, or passed out drunk in the Chiltern lockup, requiring Ellen to collect him. Joe did not know how smoothly their arrangement would work but he was determined to try. *No one steals from me.*

Waiting patiently, lost in his thoughts, a sharp tap on the door suddenly brings him from his trance.

"Joe? It's Ellen."

Springing to his feet, Joe pulls open the door, the timber scraping a track over the dry dirt.

Ellen stands, her baby wrapped tightly in a shawl around her chest, his tiny fingers curled around his face as he sucks on his thumb.

"Elly," Joe says, her name catching in his throat.

She smiles, the sunlight that glimmers through the trees falling on the ends of her hair, illuminating the blonde strands. Taking his hand, Ellen follows him into the hut.

"We have a few hours before I'll be needing to get back."

"Where is *he* today?" Joe asks.

"The races."

"I wish I could stop you from going back there."

"Please, Joe," she pleads, "let's just focus on our time together."

Joe nods, helping her unfurl the shawl as she holds her baby to her chest.

"Is that for him?" She enquires, looking to the zinc trough covered with an old woollen blanket.

"Yes. Is it suitable?"

"It'll be fine. Thank you, Joe."

Gently, she lays the sleeping baby down on the blanket, covering him with the shawl.

Joe looks down on the infant's wispy covering of dark hair.

"He won't inform on us?" he asks facetiously.

Ellen chuckles at the remark before breaking down into tears. She embraces Joe tightly, her tears dampening his cotton shirt.

"Shh, lass. Let's not spoil things with tears," he says softly, wiping them away with his thumbs.

He reaches into the pocket of his waistcoat and removes a small piece of clear topaz.

"I brought you this, I found it in Reedy Creek."

Ellen takes the stone and squeezes it in her palm.

"I'll treasure it," she replies, setting it down on the rough table.

Joe leans in and kisses her, his fingers working to remove the buttons of her dress. As it falls away from her shoulders, he notices yellow bruising on her upper arms.

"How did you get these?" He asks, his jaw set.

Ellen closes her eyes.

"He doesn't know what he's doing when he has had too much to drink."

"I've got my Da's old rifle, Elly. Just say the word."

"And what good would that bring? Him dead and you hanged?"

"I'd certainly swing easy."

Ellen slaps his shoulder.

"Joe, stop it, please."

Joe holds his arms up in surrender.

"I'm sorry. Come here," he murmurs, pulling her close.

The pair undress and Joe guides Ellen to the rough bunk and lays her down on the straw mattress. Positioning himself above her, he takes in the sight of her, his eyes settling on the raised, jagged, red streaks across her belly.

Seeing him looking at them, Ellen covers her stretchmarks self-consciously.

"They're from the baby," she says.

Joe lifts away her hand and kisses her stomach.

"You're still the most beautiful woman in all the Woolshed."

He strokes a finger down her neck and along the curves of her full breasts. He kisses her passionately, allowing his mouth to savour the taste of her skin, as her fingers grasp his hair.

Merging with her, Joe moans with pleasure as the months of separation fade.

The frame of the bunk rattles as he thrusts, the noise waking the baby, who begins to cry loudly for his mother.

Ellen turns her head in the baby's direction and attempts to quiet the cries.

"Hush...Shh."

Joe grasps her hips and squeezes his eyes shut against tears of frustration. *It can never be the same.*

"Hush now," Ellen says breathlessly, holding his face, forcing him to look at her.

Climaxing, Joe tosses his head back and groans loudly, the baby's wails piercing his ears.

"I'm sorry, Elly," he sighs, flopping beside her. "I'm not used to being made to share you."

"This is how it is now, Joe," she says, stroking his face.

"I'm aware," Joe replies, the irritation clear in his voice.

Ellen rises and moves toward her baby, picking him up to soothe him. She turns back to Joe with a frown.

"None of this was my choice, you know that, don't you?"

"Of course, I do."

She places the baby to her breast, allowing him to suckle.

"The resentment you hold is no different to mine. Only you are not trapped by it," Ellen's lip trembles, "this is my life now, Joe, and there is nothing you or I can do to change it."

Joe moves to comfort her. He enfolds her in his arms, his tears falling freely as their reality is laid bare.

***

Grasshoppers bound into Joe's shins as he works with Aaron, forking hay from the stack onto the Sherritts' dray, in preparation for its delivery to livery stable keeper George Dennett in Ford Street, Beechworth. He had spent the new year with Aaron, helping to cut and cart hay. The work had kept his limbs busy, but his mind was still caught on Ellen. He wondered how she was and whether she thought of him as much as he did her. Ned Kennedy's hut standing as a reminder of what had been and what *could* be, but Joe knew it was impossible, especially with the baby.

Forking the final leaf onto the dray, Joe sweeps up the loose blades of hay that have scattered on the ground and holds it in each palm for the two harnessed draught horses. Their large lips pluck at the hay, their bits rattling as they chew.

The lead horse, a chestnut gelding, his shoulders red raw and bleeding from the worn harness he has been worked in, twitches his muscle as a fly lands on the injured flesh. Joe eyes the straw stuffing that rubs against the horse's bloody shoulders and shakes his head pitifully. Noticing Joe's gaze, Aaron slides his hand beneath the bloodied collar. The gelding twitches and lays his ears back, threatening to bite.

"He won't pull this dray into Beechworth, Da," Aaron remarks to his father, his hand streaked with the animal's blood. "It was difficult enough yesterday driving him to Everton."

John Sherritt smacks a hand on the laden dray.

"That's four pounds of hay, boy," he declares sternly. "If not this horse, who? Ye and young Byrne? The bloody thing needs two horses to pull it."

Aaron rubs his palm against the stained fabric of his moleskins.

"I can go over and see if I can borrow a horse from James Dawson?"

John shakes his head.

"There's no time for that. It'll be raining before ye make it back with the horse."

Joe glances up at the sky at the grey summer clouds, hanging low overhead, signifying the cooling relief of rain, after days of oppressive heat.

Aaron sighs at his father's stubbornness and tugs on the bridle, but the gelding refuses to walk forward.

"How am I meant to drive them, if the bloody lead won't pull?"

"Ye've no choice," John retorts dismissively. "Carry one of the whips."

Worried that the hours of work might have been all for nothing, Joe offers up an idea.

"Do you have anything to put beneath the collar? At least that'll halt further sores."

John Sherritt mutters beneath his breath and heads toward an outbuilding, returning with a hessian sack. He shoves it towards his son.

Aaron positions the sack beneath the collar, wrapping it around the horse's shoulders.

"That should help disguise it, if nothing else," he says, frowning at his father.

Aaron climbs up onto the dray and sits on the bench seat, taking up the driving reins. He picks up a piece of hay and chews at it.

"You coming with me, Joe? I'll probably need you to help pull the dray."

Joe nods reluctantly and climbs up beside Aaron.

***

The journey into Beechworth has been a slow one, with the sack doing nothing to alleviate the pain of the hobbling gelding. As they come to the rise of Ford Street, the horse slows and finally refuses to pull, agitating the bay harnessed to the right of him.

A man driving a horse and buggy gesticulates angrily at Aaron as he overtakes the slow team.

"Christ Almighty," Aaron curses, snapping the whip on the gelding's rump, "Da will have me bloody well skinned if I don't get this lot delivered."

Despite the sting of the whip, the horse steps backwards, easing the pressure from the harness that chafes his shoulders.

"Get up!" Aaron growls, clicking his tongue.

In response, the gelding lays his ears back and stamps a hoof, the crushed granite crunching beneath his metal shoe.

Onlookers stare at the spectacle as Aaron becomes more frantic in his attempt to drive the horse on.

"You'll have to go and ask Dennett if he has a horse we can borrow to pull it," Aaron instructs, spitting the strand of hay from his mouth.

Joe scowls at him.

"I don't know why I am still getting myself involved with you, Sherritt," he replies angrily, stepping down from the cart.

Walking toward the arched entrance to George Dennett's livery stables, Joe hears the sudden sharp shrill of a whistle and notices Constable McHugh start to run in the direction of the dray. A feeling of dread overtakes him. McHugh had been the one to arrest him over the illegal use of John Phelan's lost saddle and had been the constable to later parade him into town before his six months in Beechworth Gaol. Panicked, Joe darts into a laneway and watches narrowly as McHugh runs past him.

"You there! Stop what you are about and come down from that dray!" The constable cries, as Aaron continues his vain effort of making the pained horse move forward.

Joe feels his heartbeat rise in his chest, the thumping sound filling his ears. His mouth goes dry. He wants to flee but his legs will not move, as if they are fettered to the wall. *I cannot go back inside.*

He watches as Aaron is roughly pulled from the dray and a pair of handcuffs snapped on his wrists. As he is led down the street, he pleads with the constable to allow him to make the delivery first as grey clouds release rain over Beechworth.

Joe's vision blurs, his limbs numbing as the panic attack takes hold.

VII

Joe and Aaron spread what is left of the hay in the Byrne stable, after having done the same at the Sherritt selection earlier that afternoon. The heavy downpour had soaked both the township of Beechworth and the hay, leaving it worth almost nothing. Luckily for Aaron, the magistrate, Robert Pitcairn, had acknowledged that he was not to be held accountable for the sorry condition of the horse, instead bringing into question the actions of John Sherritt and his character. Pitcairn had further declared that if John had have been driving the dray, he would have sentenced him to three months for his 'disgraceful' cruelty, rather than the five pound fine he instead imposed.

"If McHugh had allowed me to deliver the blasted stuff, we wouldn't have four pounds of hay wasted," Aaron complains, "and what bloody good were you? Cowering behind Wright's Drapery."

Joe throws the fork to the ground.

"You never bloody think," he snarls, gesturing his meaning by poking a finger into his forehead. "You see a trap coming towards you and what do you do? Attempt to run him over with the dray."

Aaron takes off his hat, using it to fan his face.

"It's too hot for fighting."

Joe rolls his eyes and follows Aaron out of the stable. The pair head to where Margaret and Mary sit beneath the Byrne veranda, with Anne and Willie Sherritt. Margaret places a dampened cloth across her forehead. The hot weather that has smothered the valley, still lingering in the afternoon shadows.

Aaron looks across at the dam.

"I think we've earnt a cool off in there," he says.

Joe follows his gaze.

"Do you think it's worth the risk?"

"What risk?"

Joe gestures to the hut of Ah On.

"Getting our limbs cut by that cranky bastard's bamboo."

Aaron laughs and slaps him on the shoulder.

"Come on, Byrne, the Chinaman can't catch the both of us."

"Alright. I'm game if you are."

Joe slips into the wash room for a linen cloth, before the pair make their way toward the dam, which had seemed like a desert mirage.

"Keep out of trouble, the two a-ye's," Anne calls from the veranda.

Walking past Ah On's hut, the aroma of steaming rice drifts on the breeze, as Ah Sin prepares the meal for himself, Ah Seong and Ah On.

Joe scans the exterior of the hut and smiles at the absence of his foe.

"No sign of Ah On."

"It wouldn't matter if there was," Aaron responds. "You say it ain't his dam?"

"No, it's not."

"Well, then, *it ain't his dam.*"

Reaching the dam, Joe stands at the bank, the scattering of trees that border it mirroring the water's surface. He undresses and wades into the water, the coldness of it startling, despite the press of hot air around him.

Joe submerges himself beneath the water and rubs away the sweat and dust that cling to his limbs. Aaron follows him in and splashes the water across his chest, stirring up the grey coloured clay with his feet.

Wading across to Joe, Aaron presses his hand on his head and dunks him under the murky water with a loud laugh.

"Buger off," Joe splutters, pushing his mate away.

Eyeing Kate playing with Margaret and Elly, Aaron stands tall in the water and stretches his arm out.

"Come and join me, Katie. It's beautiful in here."

The two girls giggle at the sight, before Kate shields their eyes.

"Looks to me like you've already got company," she replies slyly, directing the girls into the house.

Aaron pouts at the response, while Joe creeps up behind him and shoves him in the back.

"Oi, you bugger," Aaron gasps before falling into the water with a splash.

"Mullane will have you for indecent exposure," Joe jests.

Aaron rises and slaps him away

"Well if Kate ain't joining me, I'm getting out."

Joe chooses to stay in the water, savouring the cool relief. Aaron, however, climbs out, dries himself and dresses.

Sandaled feet thump over dry ground and Ah On emerges from the direction of his hut, carrying a pail to collect water for his vegetable garden.

Emboldened by Aaron's presence, Joe smacks a fist on the water's surface.

Joe mocks the new arrival.

"Oi, Ah On, look where I am! Mine! Mine!"

He thumps his chest in a parody of Ah On's earlier behaviour. Aaron sits on the bank and throws his head back, laughing loudly at the action.

"That's the way, Joe. You tell the bugger!"

Ah On stands at the bank, his face twisted with anger. The old wound that marks his forehead from his fight with Ah Fook highlighted by the sun.

"Get out! Not dam for bathing English. We use for vegetables!"

Aaron reaches for a stone and throws it in Ah On's direction. It lands with a thud in the dirt.

"It ain't your dam. Fetch your water and get lost."

Unperturbed, Ah On glares at the two young men.

"Get out or you be sorry, Ah Joe. I give you one more chance."

Joe strides toward the Chinese miner, the anger he has long felt towards the man rising fourth.

"Or what, Ah On? What will you do?" Joe gestures towards his penis, "Cut me like you did poor Ah Fook?"

The man looks savagely at Joe.

"Diu nei!" He curses.

"Oh," Joe retorts, as Ah On retreats to his hut, "Fuck me? Fuck you!"

Joe wades out of the dam, drying his dripping limbs with the linen.

"I hate that bastard."

Joe and Aaron walk up to Ah On's hut. Ah On and Ah Seong stand outside, washing clay off their feet with a wet cloth.

Aaron bends down and picks up a rock, hurling it at the bark roof. Joe laughs as the two men scatter and picks up a rock, throwing it with the same force as Aaron. The projectile bounces off the chimney.

"Tìhng dài!" Ah On yells, calling on the pair to stop. "Leave us alone!"

Aaron clutches another rock and holds it in his palm.

Ah On grabs a thick piece of bamboo that leans against the hut and rushes towards the pair, swinging it violently. Knowing the damage such a weapon can cause, especially in the hands of Ah On, Joe yanks desperately at Aaron's arm.

"Get away from him, Aaron! It's not worth it."

Ah On makes a swipe at the pair, the bamboo cutting the air with a whoosh. Joe jumps away and bolts back down towards the dam, as Aaron throws the rock he has been concealing in his palm, the jagged stone smashing into Ah On's temple, narrowly missing his eye.

Witnessing his mate's wounding, Ah Seong rushes to his side and is hastily directed to chase after Joe, while Aaron is hotly pursued by Ah On.

Adrenaline pulsing through him, Joe sprints down the creek towards the Batchelors. He weaves around sluice boxes and Chinese tents, the diggings prohibitive to gaining space. Several men who work on the creek bank look up as Joe sprints passed them. The uneven ground forcing him to slow his pace.

"Fuck off, you bastard!" Joe yells over his shoulder as the bamboo cuts across his calf.

Further up the creek, Aaron runs toward the footbridge, close to the Byrne house, Ah On still in pursuit of him. He snatches up a stick, desperate to get the miner off his tail and hurls it in Ah On's direction.

Ah On suddenly crouches down, holding his bloodied head in his hands.

"Gau mehng a!" The injured man cries.

Hearing his mate's pained calls for help, Ah Seong gives up his chase and doubles back to Ah On.

Joe slows his pace, his heart pounding in his chest. He looks back and spies Ah On crumpled on the ground, Ah Sin and Ah Seong attempting to get him to his feet.

Joe gulps the air in shock.

Aaron has killed him.

VIII

The next night, Joe paces in front of the stone hearth of Aaron's hut, a whiskey bottle grasped in his hand. Since returning to Sheepstation Creek on the night of the altercation with Ah On, the stress of the unknown had weighed heavily upon his mind. Joe swigs the bottle. *How could it all have escalated so quickly?*

He kicks at a log that sits beside the hearth. Having not seen the injured man since Saturday, Joe has no way of knowing what injuries Ah On has sustained, or indeed, how serious the injuries are. His mind constantly drifting back to the miner lying on the ground, his fingers clasped around his bloodied head.

Joe takes another mouthful of the spirit and curses as the thoughts continue to swirl. The liquor doing little to quell his anxiety. *I need opium.*

***

Entering the darkened opium den, Ah Goon welcomes Joe with a chipped-toothed smile, his long que braid wrapped around the crown of his head.

"Néih hóu, Ah Joe," the old man bows, "good see you."

"Néih hóu, Ah Goon."

Joe removes his coin purse and passes Ah Goon a sixpence and is ushered through the curtain, where the sweet, floral scent of opium smoke is exhaled by smokers who lay curled around bamboo pipes. Aware of Joe's presence, the one European of their number lifts a hand to his face, the action slowed by the mellowing effect of the opium, in an attempt to obscure his identity.

Many of the Europeans who smoke opium, do not wish to be seen indulging in this "heathen Chinee" habit, especially when the local *Ovens and Murray Advertiser* drilled into its readers that such a "social evil" should not be tolerated in any "Christian country." Accusing the Chinese of being "degraded beings," who "smoke opium, thieve, gamble and loaf," but as Ah King had pointed out in his *letter to the editor*, "change the phrase 'smoke opium' to 'drink whisky' and the epithet will apply much more forcibly to the European population." Such anti-Chinese sentiment has never sat well with Joe. He knows he is not above them, and so does not feel he is tarnishing his reputation by being seen within their camps and opium dens.

Joe positions himself on the wooden bunk, while Ah Goon prepares the pipe. He lays a silver tea tray down, the opium pipe and lamp resting upon it.

"M̀hgòi," Joe acknowledges in thanks.

Holding the ceramic bowl of the pipe over the lamp, Joe places it to his lips and sucks the vapourised opium through the stem of the pipe, filling his lungs. The drug's relaxing effect washing over him.

***

The much-needed anxiety relief Joe had been provided by the opium vapours lasted only as long as Joe was in Ah Goon's den, and had all but dissipated upon his arrival back at the hut. Each day he expects to hear the familiar thud of police boots and the clattering of a fist brought upon the door. The unknowns of Ah On's condition and what trouble it will bring him has been like a noose around his neck, the knot drawing tighter with each passing day. Aaron, however, has shown little concern, believing that everything would be alright, as he always did.

"Have you seen the Chinaman about?" Joe asks, from his position on an upturned apple crate.

Aaron shakes his head and continues kneading damper. He rolls it into a sausage shape and coils it around a stick before holding it over the fire in the fireplace.

"He is probably off sulking somewhere."

Joe glares at Aaron.

"Did you not see him get up?"

"I didn't see anything, Joe. I hoofed it as fast as you did. Did *you* see him get up?"

"No," he utters. "Fucking hell, Aaron, you've probably killed him."

"Don't *you* accuse me of murder. You started it with all your bloody blowing."

Joe jumps from the crate.

"*You* were the one who caved his bloody head in with a rock!"

Aaron squeezes the damper to see if it is cooked, and then pulls it off the stick and tosses it onto a chipped plate.

"Oi, it wasn't that bad," Aaron answers, defensively. "Would have been a damn sight worse if he'd taken to us with the bamboo."

"Bugger this," Joe spits, grasping his sac coat and hat from the bunk.

"Where the hell are you going?" Aaron asks through a mouth of half chewed damper.

"As far away from you as possible. Not everything is a God damn lark, and you know as well as I do that we're both going to be lagged for this."

"So, what's the use of worrying?" Aaron shrugs, unconcerned. "The traps will come, arrest us, and we'll tell them what happened."

Joe curses at Aaron's indifference and yanks open the door.

***

Determined to find out Ah On's condition, Joe travels back to the Sebastopol Chinese camp for answers. Singling out Meng Ye, a miner who was friendly with Ah On, Joe approaches the man, who is bent at the creek bank, slowly pouring a bucket of sediment along the steady flow of water of the sluice. Hearing movement behind him, the man whirls around, clutching a piece of bamboo.

"No thief! No thief!" The miner shouts, waving the bamboo.

Joe throws his arms up to show he has no bad intentions.

"Meng Ye, it's me, Ah Joe."

The man focuses on Joe with a look of doubt.

"Ah Joe?"

"Hai," Joe nods pointing to his chest. "Ngóh giujouh, Ah Joe."

Meng Ye places the bucket of sediment on the bank.

"What you want?"

"Has Ah On been at the camp?"

The miner shakes his head.

"Ah On in hospital. Got hurt by English."

"How do you know that?"

Meng Ye points further down the creek in the direction of James Chappell's Reidford Hotel.

"Ah Jim from hotel read in paper."

Joe feels the tightness in his chest slightly dissipate, *at least he is still alive.*

***

Entering the dimly lit bar of the Reidford, Joe is greeted by the polite smile of Cornishman James Chappell while he rubs a rag in the inside of a glass.

"Hullo, Joe. Be liking a drink, would ya, my 'andsome?"

While James was seen by many of the locals as a 'grumpy old devil,' Joe had always managed to stay on his good side.

"I can never refuse a drink," Joe acknowledges, "but what I am actually after is yesterday's paper, if you have it?"

James crosses his arms across his chest.

"Is this about young Sherritt troublin' Ah On?"

Joe nods, feeling a sense of shame. A man who was lost in the head of his ale suddenly looks up, interested in the conversation. Joe turns his back on the nosey drunk and leans closer to James.

"Aye," he answers quietly.

"Alright," James responds, "I'll fetch ya something to drink and then I'll get the paper. What'll it be?"

"A nobbler of whiskey, please."

James reaches for a bottle and pours the spirit. He slides Joe the drink and reaches under the bar for the January 16th copy of the *Ovens and Murray Advertiser.*

"You're lucky, I was just about to use it to get the fire started."

Joe swigs the whiskey and scans the pages of the paper. Coming to page two, his narrowed light blue eyes fall on the report he is looking for.

'Murderous Assault. — Yesterday, a Chinaman named Ah Hong, a miner residing at Sebastopol, was admitted into the Ovens District Hospital, suffering from a dangerous wound in the face. Upon examination, Dr Farr found that the zygomatic arch, or what scientific men would call the cheekbone, was broken into five pieces. The wound is a horrible one, and the patient lies in a dangerous state. From what we can learn, the wound was inflicted by a stone thrown at the Chinaman, who bears the character of being a harmless fellow, by Mr Aaron Sherritt, of Sheep Station Creek. We have not heard full particulars, but from what we can learn, the assault was a most unprovoked and murderous one.'

Joe's hand rubs at his forehead as the words take effect. Feeling his heart rate rise, Joe knocks back the liquor in a single swig and excuses himself, a feeling of nausea washing over him. Stumbling around the side of the hotel, he doubles over and vomits.

IX

For the past four weeks, Joe has been holed up in Aaron's hut. The crippling anxiety he has felt, rendering him almost useless. He knows the police will eventually come to arrest the pair of them and, depending on whether Ah On succumbs to his injuries, that charge could be murder. The news report he had read at Chappell's hotel had been locked in his mind, the words as clear as if he had read it only yesterday. It had been stated that the rock that had struck the miner had broken his cheekbone into five pieces, this was dangerous enough for the man, but if Aaron's aim had been slightly higher, he would have been killed instantly.

Aaron had laughed off Joe's unease, shrugging his shoulders with his usual self-assuredness. Rather than spending his days locked away worrying, he had picked up work bark stripping in the hills of El Dorado. Joe envied his mate's ability to shrug off trouble, but for him it was simply not possible. He stewed obsessively, unable to see anything beyond his fears.

Picking up the small mirror, Joe wipes away the smudgy fingerprints with his sleeve and holds it aloft. He stares back at his reflection; purple bags darken his eyes, his face slightly gaunt from stress. With no one to express his thoughts to, Joe opens his journal, and takes out a pencil.

I wish I was away from here, away from Aaron and all this damned trouble. I promised myself I would never again allow him to put me away, but what good has it done me? Maybe a gaol cell is all I am good for. Opium and whiskey has done nothing to ease my worrying. I want Elly...

Joe's thoughts trail off. He presses the lead into the paper and snaps the nib.

***

The day of the 5th of February stretches into evening and Joe awaits Aaron's return. The summer sunset is ablaze with burnt orange and crimson coalescing. He takes out his watch for the third time and checks it nervously - eight o'clock. *He should have returned two hours ago.* Joe begins to panic and paces in front of the window, a heightened sense of dread consumes him.

***

Early the next morning, Joe is awoken suddenly by the heavy pounding of a fist on the door, the force of it rattling the small hut. He gasps and rushes toward the window. Looking narrowly out of it, he spies Mounted-constable Mullane glowering back at him.

"Ye best be opening this door, Byrne," he orders.

Joe freezes. He considers breaking out of the hut with the axe that rests beside the hearth but quickly composes himself as Mullane's voice booms from outside.

"I said open up!"

Joe pulls the door open and is met with a rebuke.

"In future, I suggest ye be quicker in opening the door," the constable orders. He removes a warrant from his pocket and thrusts it at Joe. "Joseph Byrne, I have a warrant here for yer arrest for maliciously wounding one Ah On. Do ye have anything to say on the matter? And I must caution ye to mind what ye say."

Joe feels himself trembling. Having faltered under Mullane's interrogation previously when they met, he knows he must not repeat the mistake this time. He clears his throat and straightens.

"I have nothing to say; I did not do it, or see it done."

Mullane's eyes narrow.

"Were ye with Aaron Sherritt on the 13th of January?"

Joe's mind blanks at that date. It was a Saturday in January, that is all he can remember.

"I don't know if it was the 13th, but I was there the day the Chinaman got hurt."

Hearing enough, the constable removes the handcuffs and clasps them around Joe's wrists. He is led out of the hut and told to wait beside his horse, while he unfurls a rope from the cantle of the saddle and ties it around the metal chain of the handcuffs. Mullane mounts and edges his horse forward into a walk with a jab of his spurs.

***

Joe is led down Ford Street behind Mullane's horse. Feeling ashamed, he keeps his head lowered, focused on the worn toes of his blucher boots.

Arriving at the Government Camp, Mullane dismounts in the police paddock and unties the rope from the handcuffs. He glances up at Joe with a perplexed expression.

"It is strange," he begins, sarcastically. "Ye say ye were there, and yet ye seem to know nothing of the assault."

Joe clenches his jaw. His anxiety surpassed by derision

"It occurred in this way; we were bathing in the dam and the

Chinaman ran after us. Aaron ran one way and I ran the other. *I saw nothing at all of it.*"

"Ye will have a chance to tell that to Mr. Brown tomorrow," he replies, pushing Joe into the gloomy lockup.

He eyes the two wooden buckets in the corner. *Thank Christ I am alone.*

***

After a sleepless night in the small Beechworth lockup, Joe is brought before Mr. Brown J.P and charged with 'inflicting grievous bodily harm on one Ah On at Sebastopol, by throwing stones and striking him on the head.' The justice of the peace remands him for a week inside Beechworth Gaol. Joe feels his blood run cold; *I am going back inside.* He wants to thump his hand against the wood of the dock and scream his innocence. It was Aaron! *It is always Aaron!*

***

Entering the remand yard, Joe looks for Aaron in the group of men and finds him sitting alone along the wooden bench, scraping a fingernail into the crusted dust that coats his hat brim.

He glances upwards as Joe approaches.

"I see they found you too. Constable McCracken got me while I was bark stripping."

Joe sits down but does not answer. His jaw set.

"You not speaking?" Aaron enquires.

Joe looks away from him and focuses on a boy who looks no older than thirteen, his face marred with a blackened eye. He paces the length of the yard, scuffing his worn wellington boots over the slabs of granite. The sound compounding Joe's frustration.

"Do you not see where we are? You got us bloody well lagged again."

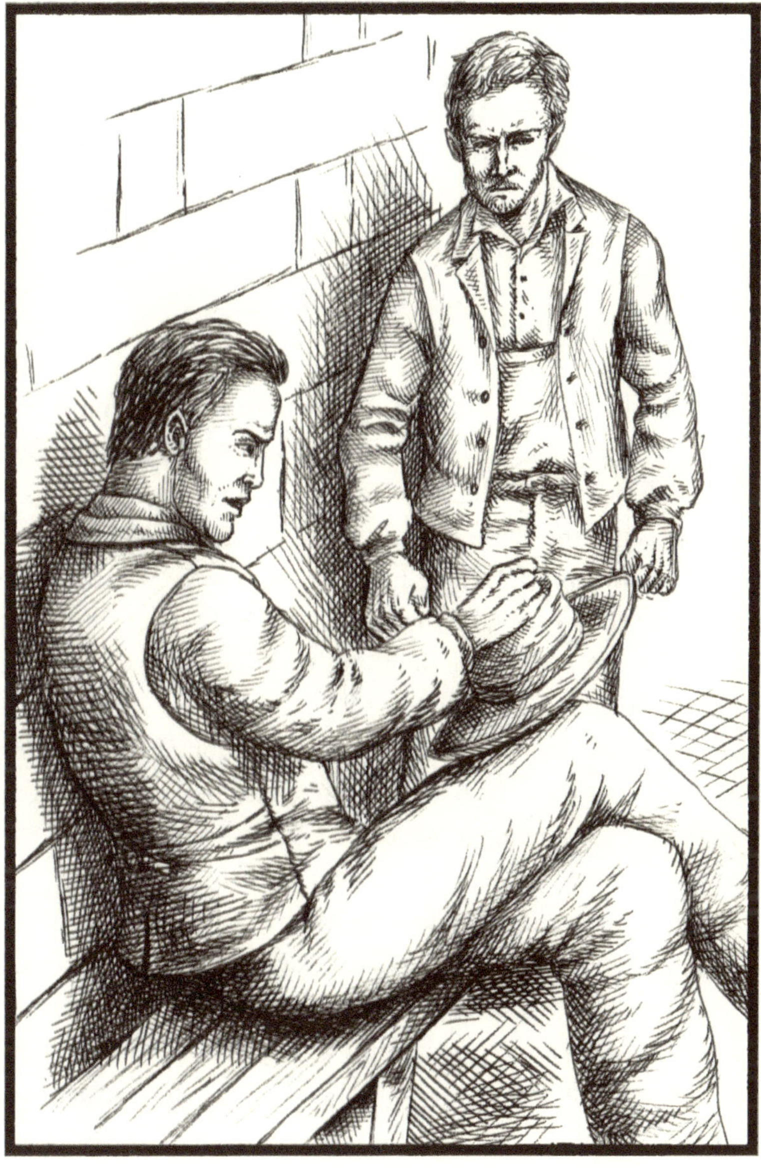

Aaron huffs at the accusation and places his hat back on his head.

"Ease up, Byrne. You've made your damn point."

Joe scowls and shifts irritably on the bench, conscious that his life is in an ever-repeating cycle of trouble. He stands abruptly and moves towards the large table in the centre of the yard and sits down, his back turned against Aaron.

***

Joe lies awake, tossing and turning uncomfortably on the thin piece of matting that serves as a bed. He rakes a hand through his sweat tangled hair and kicks away the woollen blanket, cursing against the heat that is trapped in the cell. He looks up at the small window pitifully, he would do anything for some fresh air to escape the pungent smell that rises from the contents of the bucket. The milky beam of moonlight illuminating Aaron's hair as he slumbers, air whistling from his nose. *The bugger would sleep through anything.*

Beside him, a fellow remand prisoner stirs and mutters. Standing up, the man staggers toward the bucket and relieves himself, the pronounced splashing sound causing Joe to wince.

"You've just pissed in the fucking water bucket," he snarls.

The man merely grunts and lays back on his piece of matting.

Resisting the urge to pour the bucket over the offending scoundrel, Joe rolls onto his side and scrunches his eyes closed. He imagines the look on Aaron's face as he knocks back a pannikin of tainted water first thing in the morning and manages a thin smile at Aaron's expense.

***

On the 13th of February, after a long week spent in remand, Joe and Aaron are escorted from the gaol to the Beechworth Courthouse, where they are brought before Magistrate Robert Pitcairn and charged with 'assaulting one Ah On at the Woolshed with the intent to do grievous bodily harm.'

With the police court assembled, Ah On is guided to the stand and for the first time since that fateful evening, Joe is finally made aware of the injuries the man has sustained at Aaron's hand. The miner's cheek is sunken and stained with a deep purple bruise. A collection of stitches marking the area where the shattered pieces of bone had been removed from his face.

The clerk of the court begins by reciting the oath, with Ah On blowing out a match, the Chinese equivalent of swearing on the Bible.

Ah On clears his throat and glances briefly toward the dock, his eyes locking on Joe. Unable to look him in the eye, Joe focusses on the white of his knuckles as his hands grip the walnut-coloured wood of the dock.

"I am miner living at Sebastopol," he begins. "I have lived there many years. There is dam and garden near my hut. I was working in garden on 13th January. I saw Byrne in dam. Sherritt was there too, but still was wearing clothes. Byrne called me to look at him in water and Sherritt threw a stone, but it not hit me. I walked away to my hut where my mates were. Byrne and Sherritt followed me and threw stones at us."

The incident swirls in Joe's head, as the miner continues his description. On hearing that Ah On is still a patient of the Ovens District Hospital, a month on from the fray, Joe is rattled, while Aaron raises his brow in surprise realising the seriousness of the wound he had inflicted.

There is further evidence from the prosecution, with Ah On's two mates, Ah Seong and Ah Sin detailing Joe and Aaron's attack on their hut. Dr. Fox, details the extent of Ah On's injuries and Mounted-constable Mullane describes Joe's arrest, muddling the date. "*Ye say ye were there, and yet ye seem to know nothing about it*," Joe broods to himself, repeating the sarcasm uttered by the policeman at the time of his arrest. *Bloody snob.* Finally, Constable McCracken who gives the particulars as to Aaron's arrest and statement.

Telling the court, "I arrested the prisoner Sherritt on the morning of the 5th about 5 miles from El Dorado, towards Chiltern, on the warrant produced. Told him the charge, and cautioned him. He said, 'I admit the charge; he ran after me and struck me first, and I then struck him with a stick.'"

For the defence, Margaret and Mary Byrne and Anne and Willie Sherritt are called to give evidence, with Joe feeling apprehensive at what she will recount. *Will she again paint me as the failed son?*

Margaret emerges from the witnesses' room and walks down to the witness box, the floorboards squeaking under her tread. Picking up the Bible she holds it aloft.

"I swear by Almighty God, to tell the truth, the whole truth and nothing but the truth."

She is asked if she remembers the evening of the 13th of January and nods.

"I remember the evening the Chinaman was hurt. I Saw the Chinaman running after Sherritt with a bamboo, and hit him a couple of times. Sherritt picked up a stick and threw it at the Chinaman. It struck the Chinaman on the side of the head and knocked him down."

"What side was complainant struck?" Sergeant Barber asks.

"I cannot say what side of the head the Chinaman was struck. They were about 37 feet from where I was, which was about 50 yards from the Chinaman's hut. It was Ah On that was struck," she responds, the tone of her County Clare accent is firm, but there is a softness to her words, the resentment no longer apparent.

"Who was there besides yourself?" Begins Mr. Brown.

"Mrs. Sherritt and my children were there."

"Did you witness the actions of complainant's friends?"

"The other Chinaman chased my son for about 200 yards, and then went back. The Chinaman was calling out for Ah On, and picked up Ah On's stick. The Chinaman that ran after my son picked up Ah On's stick and the stick Sherritt threw at Ah On, besides his own."

After the evidence of Ann Sherritt, Aaron's brother Willie is called, almost tripping on the step of the box in his haste, before fumbling for the Bible to commence the oath. Once he finishes recounting what he had witnessed, he turns to Sergeant Barber, his cheeks flushed.

"I...I heard the witnesses ordered out of court this morning," the 13-year-old stammers, "but I stayed and was in court while my mother and Mrs. Byrne gave evidence."

Magistrate Pitcairn sighs at the boy's incompetence.

"I cannot now refuse to take the evidence you have put forward, but it will not be worth much. When you next find yourself in this court, leave when instructed."

"Bloody Willie," Aaron grumbles quietly, "thick as they come."

A common Sherritt trait, Joe thinks to himself.

At the conclusion of Mary Byrne's evidence, which is similar to that given by Margaret, Magistrate Pitcairn commits Joe and Aaron for trial at the next Court of General Sessions, which is to be heard on the 28th of February. Bail is offered to the pair for £50 each. A large sum for the impoverished families and Joe knows a week of respite out of gaol is far beyond his reach.

"That didn't go too badly, apart from Willie's daftness" Aaron remarks, as they enter the small holding cell behind the dock. "Even your old mother seemed to be on our side."

Joe nods, still taken aback by her changed demeanour.

"She's never liked Ah On," he replies, attempting to find the answer for the change.

Without any more time to process it, their solicitors, William Zincke and Frederick Brown, enter the cell and Joe is pulled aside by Mr. Zincke, his movements hurried.

"Joseph, would you have the required amount for bail? I appreciate it is a high sum, but I'm sure you'll be wanting some respite from your cell, and of course, it will look better in the eyes of the Magistrate."

Joe shudders as he thinks of the men he has been locked up with, but with insufficient funds to his name, there is no other option but to be sent back to remand.

"What I have would hardly make a dent in it."

Mr. Zincke smiles mournfully, in an attempt to show understanding for Joe's position. Even though Joe knows the solicitor cannot possibly comprehend what it is like to merely survive.

"Would you like me to speak with your family; they may be able to offer some help?"

As Joe contemplates the idea, Aaron suddenly elbows him in the side.

"I have a little coin saved, Joe, and Da will help. Besides, he still owes you for the work you did around the selection."

Joe raises an eyebrow at his mate's sudden charity.

"Are you sure?"

"Consider us square," he replies, before turning back to Mr. Brown gesturing for him to write a note. "Tell my father to look beneath my bunk. He'll find an old kerosene can under it with a decent amount of coin in it," Aaron pauses and winks over his shoulder at Joe. "Profit from old Mr. Phelan."

"Alright, I will pass that on, Mr. Sherritt," the solicitor affirms.

The two men leave the holding cell, their polished boots echoing along the passage as they return to the courtroom.

Joe clears his throat and turns to Aaron.

"Thanks, mate."

Aaron brushes a hand through his neatly combed hair.

"As I said before, consider us square."

***

That evening in the remand cell, Joe sits on the coconut matting, gazing wistfully up at the small window; the promise of freedom awaiting him on the other side. Before he and Aaron had returned to the gaol, they had been informed their families would be doing everything they could to secure bail.

This news had come as a shock to Joe, the large sum seemed far out of his family's reach. While he knew John Sherritt would always come to the aid of Aaron, or at least do his best to, such an act was never a given with Margaret. However, in their fight with Ah On, mother and son had a common enemy and in rallying around Joe, Margaret was making more than just a stand for herself and for her son, but the other inhabitants of Sebastopol whose attempts to use the dam had been thwarted by the miner. '*The dam belongs to no one,*' she had defiantly declared to the court, and while a verdict was still to be reached, Joe at least felt a sense of optimism as to the future of their relationship.

X

On the morning of the 16th of February, Joe and Aaron are informed that their bail has been paid and they will finally be leaving remand.

The other prisoners watch dejectedly as the pair are led out of the yard in preparation for their release. Entering the Beechworth Police Station, Joe and Aaron are read the terms of their bail by an older constable who wears a pair of Pince-nez spectacles, the eyewear resting precariously on the bridge of his nose. While engaged in reading the document, the spectacles slip off his nose and land with a thud on the table, causing the constable to pause to readjust them, much to the bemusement of Aaron, who stands beside Joe attempting to conceal his smirk.

With one final readjustment of his spectacles, the man slides the bonds across to the pair to sign. Joe dips the nib into the small clay inkwell and holds the pen firmly, signing the bail bond in a quick and confident manner. Meanwhile, Aaron scrawls his name laboriously, struggling to form the letters of his name.

"I'm no scholar," Aaron explains, as a way of excuse.

"No matter," the constable replies, sweeping the two documents into his hands and securing them beneath a lump of quartz as a paperweight. "As long as it's signed."

Stepping out of the station, Joe savours the warmth of the sun on his face. After two weeks spent in the claustrophobic dinginess of Beechworth Gaol, it has been a long-awaited sensation. The pair begin their journey home along Sydney Road, the Vine Hotel shining like a beacon ahead of them.

***

Having decided to spend the eight days before his return to court at his mother's selection, Joe has spent his time replacing the rotting fence posts of the horse paddock, a job he had been promising to complete since before his six months in gaol the previous year. His decision to return home was one he felt only right, especially after the large amount of money Margaret had managed to scrape together for his release from remand. Joe had also hoped the work would serve as a distraction from the dark reality he was still caught in, but it had done the opposite, with the monotonous work allowing his mind free to shift between thoughts of his painful loss of Ellen and the possibility of another six months in prison greys. He quivers at the memory of the unbearable itchiness of the wool.

Rubbing away the goosepimples that rise along his forearms, Joe places the final sapling post into the ground and shovels the mound of soil around it, compacting the dry earth with a stamp of his boot. Wiping away the sweat that glistens across his forehead, his ears catch on the grumbling that sounds from the direction of Ah On's hut. He notices Ah Sin weaving his way around the mining race, a large sack of flour slung across his shoulder.

"Do you need help?" Joe calls, pointing to the sack, hoping the gesture will serve as a small peace offering.

Ah Sin looks up from under the brim of his conical hat, attempting to identify the owner of the voice. Realising it has come from Joe, his face scrunches into a scowl.

"Pūk gāa!" The stooped man curses, "Don't want help from you! Go annoy another poor Chinaman!"

"Only trying to help," Joe offers, watching as Ah Sin kicks open the door of the hut, the motion causing it to bang loudly against the slab wall, startling a sulphur crested cockatoo that is perched on the roof.

Joe watches while the screeching bird disappears behind the range and bends down to pick up the railing, securing each end into the notches he has chopped into the post, an unwanted feeling of guilt tugging at his heart. With Ah On still in hospital, Ah Sin and Ah Seong had been left to take up the work of the injured man, which had added to their resentment. His fight had never been with them, but now it inevitably was.

While Ah On's mates had shown Joe mistrust, he had found himself being shown an equal amount of support and condemnation from the residents of the Woolshed Valley. Some were understanding of how such an incident could escalate, aware of the miner's behaviour regarding the dam. Similarly, the Chinese who treated Ah On as an outcast, saw it as justice for Ah Fook. While others were outraged by the violence that had been meted out to the usually quiet Chinese by two young larrikins. One person who had notably withheld their support for Joe was James Salisbury. How much of this was being used by the man as further justification for his tearing apart of the relationship between Joe and his daughter, Ellen, Joe did not know. *A drifter with no future*, James had called him, and with the prospect of another prison sentence present looming, Joe realised he was fulfilling that prophecy. *Perhaps she is better off without me?* Feeling a lump rise in his throat, he pushes the thought to the back of his mind and turns his attention back to the unfinished fence.

XI

It is the last day of February, and the morning light shines brightly through the chinks of the hut, signalling the arrival of Joe and Aaron's day back in court.

Joe stirs in his bed and stretches, his brother Denny slumbering beside him, mumbling incoherently as he dreams. Rising, he begins dressing into his Sunday best of brown tweed trousers, brown vest, and jacket, and a crisp white shirt, with a paper collar pinned around the neckline. After pulling on his blucher boots, he brushes a wooden comb through his hair, and the short beard he has allowed to grow. He washes his face, the water stinging his sunburnt cheeks.

Walking out into the front room, Joe's gaze falls on the figure of Aaron, who lies coiled, like a dog, close to the hearth. He nudges him with the toe of his boot.

"Wake up, Aaron."

The dozing man rolls onto his back and swats a hand against Joe's shin.

"Bugger off, I've almost got her corset unhooked."

Joe rolls his eyes. He bends down and slaps him across the ear.

"We've got to be in Beechworth by nine o'clock."

Aaron sits up with a mutter and takes out his fob watch, holding it close to his face with a squint.

"There's plenty of time."

"Just get yourself ready. I won't have you making us late."

"I don't know any cove who insists on being places as early as you."

"Maybe if you were, you'd have gotten that lass's corset off hours ago," Joe answers slyly.

Aaron goes to answer, but Margaret's entry silences his retort.

"Yer both ready, then?"

"Well, one of us is," Joe replies, making a point of glancing down at his dishevelled looking mate. Margaret is still dressed in her work clothes.

"Mary and meself will be seeing yer both in court later."

Aaron gestures to Mary.

"Do you remember what we told you to say?"

The girl sighs and nods, having learnt the evidence by rote.

"You and Joe were bathing in the dam, when Ah On came and ordered you out," Mary begins, her voice a drone. "His two friends then came out with sticks and ran after you and Joe. There was no blood on Ah On's face until he fell and both you and Joe were bleeding on the arms from the blows you were given with the bamboo."

"Good girl," Aaron smiles, ruffling her hair.

"The poor girl will be remembering it for the rest of her life," Margaret says, stirring a pot of porridge that hangs over the fire.

"It's alright," Mary begins, "Aaron promised to buy me some boiled lollies from Paddy Allen's store for my trouble."

Margaret frowns.

"Yer bribing my child, Sherritt?"

Aaron laughs and pours himself a pannikin of tea.

"Have to make it worth her while, don't I?"

"Let's hope this is the end of it," Margaret sighs.

"Of course it will be," Aaron says with a chuckle, glancing across at Joe.

Joe is not so sure.

***

Joe and Aaron walk towards the stable in preparation for their ride to Beechworth. Joe is dressed in his Sunday best, and Aaron in his usual mismatched attire with added soot from the hearth covering his polka dot sleeve.

Joe glances sideward at his mate with a raise of his eyebrow.

"Is there a reason you chose last night to sleep beside the hearth? You look like a bloody chimney sweep."

As if suddenly conscious of the soot on his arm, Aaron begins rubbing at it, however it has little effect, except to work it deeper into the cotton fabric. He spits into his palm and tries again, before shrugging his shoulders in defeat.

"It would probably have helped our case if you had at least tried to look presentable."

"We can't all be looking like a bank clerk, Byrne," he answers dismissively, taking his jacket which lies across his saddle and puts it on. "Satisfied?"

Joe sneers but withholds his reply.

***

Entering the township of Beechworth, Joe and Aaron's pace is abruptly halted by a herd of cattle being driven by four stockmen, the beasts destined for the saleyards of Gray and Co. The sudden encounter agitates Music, who begins prancing, her teeth grinding against the metal of the bit.

Aware of their presence, the rear rider glances over his shoulder at the pair, his face concealed by a fly veil tied around the brim of his hat.

"In a hurry lad?" He asks.

Joe nods, loosening his reins as Music begins impatiently pawing at the crushed granite of the road.

The stockman places his fingers to his lips and whistles a high-pitched tune, which is soon answered by the lead, who raises his arm.

"Pass wide," the man directs.

"Thank you," Joe acknowledges, touching the brim of his hat.

Pressing his thighs against Music's side, he edges her into a trot, her ears laid back as she passes the herd.

***

Having finally arrived at the police station, the pair dismount and are led to the lockup by a short middle-aged constable.

"She's full today, boys," the constable sneers, a purple bruise visible beneath blonde whiskers that cover his cheeks.

Joe glances ahead at the granite building, bathed in sunlight, and cringes, dreading the stench that awaits him.

As they approach, a guard who has been standing beneath the shade of the overhang of the roof stands to attention, the array of keys jingling in his hand as he locates the correct one and slides it into the lock.

"It's a pity you won't be joining us," Aaron says to the constable as the guard pulls the lockup door ajar.

"You looking for more trouble? You won't feel so smart after a day spent sweating in here."

Aaron sniggers at the comeback and is roughly pushed through the narrow doorway for his trouble, with Joe given the same treatment, his bluchers scraping over the granite step, the door quickly slams behind him with a thud. His eyes adjust to the gloom and settle on ten other men who stare, miserably, back at the pair, a musky smell permeates the air.

With the wooden bench taken by the other men, Joe sits himself down on the floor beside a boy who appears no older than fifteen, his willowy frame concealed by little more than rags, with the threadbare trousers held at the waist with a piece of tattered rope, the ends peeking beneath the waistcoat. The boy's long fingers curl protectively around the brim of the porkpie hat in his lap as he glances across at Joe and Aaron, his blue eyes darting over them warily.

Joe smiles and stretches his legs out, while Aaron remains standing, his jacket snags against the rough bricks of granite as he leans against it.

"My name's Joe," he greets, holding out his hand.

The boy brushes his hair from his face and smiles slightly, but does not respond.

"I won't bite," Joe jests, aware of the boy's hesitancy, "although, I can't answer for the cove that was brought in with me."

The boy laughs nervously at the remark and takes Joe's hand, his palm clammy.

"I'm Dan."

Aaron looks down on the raggedy dressed boy with a sneer, his eyebrows raising as he notices the twine that holds his boots together.

"They lag you for vagrancy?"

The remark earns a snigger from the other men in the lockup. Joe glares at them.

"Ignore him," Joe says, focussing his attention back on Dan.

"They think it upsets me, but I'm used to it," Dan pauses and pulls at a loose thread on his sleeve, "have to be."

Joe looks at the threadbare suit; the loose style of trousers and sac coat fashionable during the late 1860's, but now a clear mark of the boy's poverty.

"I take it you're the youngest brother?"

The boy nods.

"My brother Ned wore them before me, but they were bought for my uncle Jim." Dan holds up the hat, "This is the hat Ned wore while bushranging with Harry Power. We call it the "Harry hat."

Joe ponders the name, it sounds familiar.

"Ned Kelly?"

On the connection being made, Dan sits up straight against the wall, a look of pride etched across his face. He passes the hat to Joe to look at, the action causing Aaron to smirk.

"What got you lagged?" Joe asks, running his fingers over the rough felt.

"I've been accused of stealing a saddle from a man in Benalla."

Joe hands the hat back.

"Accused? You didn't lift it?"

The question is met with a look of offence.

"No, I paid for it proper. Even have a receipt for the sale. But an old dodger in Benalla mistook mine for his and accused me of stealing it." Dan stares wistfully at the floor, "the traps are always looking for reasons to slap the darbies on us. They hang around my Ma's selection like flies."

"It'd be nice to cut the long noses from their faces to keep them from sniffing around," Joe replies with a wink.

The statement causes Dan's eyes to widen.

"This isn't your first time in trouble?"

"Can't you tell he's a hardened criminal," Aaron interjects sarcastically.

Joe ignores the jibe and shakes his head.

"No, I've been in here before," he pauses and gestures toward Aaron, "this bastard's got me lagged twice."

Aaron rolls his eyes.

"Ah yes, you had no will of your own," he snaps.

The oppressive heat in the cell, coupled with Aaron's remark, causes Joe to bristle irritably.

"You know damn well the way of it."

"Do I?" Aaron asks, leaning forward to prod Joe in the shoulder, "Why don't *you* tell the kid who it was that molested the poor little Chinaman. Oh, that's right, it was big brave Joey Byrne."

Joe slaps his hand away, causing Aaron to laugh mockingly.

"Look kid, I know he dresses respectable, but he ain't no better than me. If you had a decent horse out there, he'd have it lifted before you knew what happened."

Without hesitation, Joe jumps to his feet and grabs his hands around Aaron's throat, his teeth bared. He wishes for nothing more than to plant a fist in his jaw and silence him.

"Some excitement lads," one of the men says, rubbing his hands together in anticipation.

Aaron grins provocatively at Joe's fury.

"One of us will be leaving here with a broken nose, and you know it won't be me."

"Let's see how mouthy you are with no teeth," Joe snarls, their eyes locked in animalistic rage. Joe pounds a fist into Aaron's stomach, sending him back against the wall. He attempts to conceal the wind Joe has taken out of him with a smirk.

The men jeer at the action, spoiling for excitement in the claustrophobic space.

Dan roughly grabs Joe's shoulder and pulls him away, his strength hidden by his oversized clothes, as the guard raps a baton on the cell door.

"Oi! Quiet in there!"

Joe shrugs off Dan's grip and looks squarely at Aaron.

"You better hope we're let off. Or I'll be breaking more than your teeth."

"Oh, I'll be getting off," Aaron boasts, straightening his waistcoat, "they can't pin me for anything."

Dan shoots Aaron daggers.

"Is he always such a loud mouth."

"Aye," Joe mutters resentfully.

***

After a long and stifling day spent awaiting their hearing, Joe and Aaron are finally called and arranged behind the dock. The Jury is called, but given the late hour of the afternoon, an adjournment is called for the following morning.

***

Grumbling, Joe leads Music from the police paddock and across the road to the stables of the Albion Hotel.

"It's been a long day. I'm desperate for a drink."

The pair enter the smoke hazed-bar room, where publican Ferdinand Heuss leans on his elbows talking to a drinker while the barmaid moves about behind him in a flustered state.

"Always chewing some poor chap's ear off," Aaron asserts, nodding to the publican. Mr. Heuss was notorious for his ability to talk, with a simple greeting often ending into an hour of conversation. He was well versed in current events, which no amount of polite fob watch inspecting could ease.

"Probably been there for hours," Joe remarks, thankful it's not him bailed up.

Careful to avoid eye contact with Mr. Heuss, Joe and Aaron stand a little back from the bar and order two nobblers of whiskey.

Taking a swig, Joe sighs as it tingles against his gums, his ears pricking as a voice sounds behind him.

"Fancy seeing you in here, Joe."

Turning around, Joe's eyes fall on Dan, who is accompanied by a taller man, with dark hair and beard, dressed in a red and black Rob Roy tartan shirt, dark trousers and vest which is covered by a light tweed jacket. His heavy eyebrows furrowed slightly as he looks back at Joe and Aaron.

"Did you get off?" Dan asks, with a smile.

"Won't know until tomorrow morning. I take it you were discharged?" Joe replies, his eyes falling to the man's hobnail boots, which despite being the boot favoured by labouring men, look flash beside Dan's beaten pair.

The boy reaches into his pocket and pulls out a crinkled piece of paper, and waves it triumphantly.

"You should have seen their faces when they saw I had a receipt. The Magistrate said I had no reason to be there."

"I bet it was a picture."

As if suddenly remembering he isn't alone, Dan gestures eagerly to the man beside him.

"Joe, Aaron, this is my brother, Ned."

"Good to meet you Joe, Aaron," Ned says, shaking their hands, the quietness of his voice taking Joe off guard.

"Likewise, Ned. I've never met a bushranger before," he grins with a wink.

Ned takes a swig of his ale, the foam caught in the red flecked hairs of his moustache, which he wipes away with the back of his hand.

"A bushranger?" He asks guardedly.

"Aye, weren't you with Harry Power?"

"A lot of people think I gave him up. I was treated like a damned black snake, even by my relations."

Dan shifts uneasily and stares into his ale.

"I'm not one to believe all I read," Joe responds.

"He was a cranky old bugger, but I never gave him up. Anyway, I'm honest these days."

Aaron scoffs at the remark.

"How can a man live an honest life in times like these?"

The question touches a nerve, causing Ned's expression to harden.

"It does my Ma no good to have me rotting in gaol. If I can't live an honest life what good am I to anyone?"

"I agree, Ned," Joe declares, looking sidelong at Aaron, who mutters into his whiskey. "Times are tough, but they're a damn sight worse in gaol, as Aaron and myself can both attest."

Ned places his finished glass down on the bar and nods towards his brother.

"Danny said you found yourself some trouble with a Chinaman?"

"That's right."

"I had a run in with a beggar named Ah Fook several years ago. He threatened my sister, so I taught him a lesson. I snatched that bamboo right out of his hand and thrashed him with it."

Joe and Aaron exchange glances.

"Joe knew an Ah Fook. The poor fellow was found lying dead in the bush without his balls."

The graphic detail causes Dan to splutter into his beer. Ned winces.

"You friendly with the Mongolians?"

Joe nods.

"My mother's selection is on the Sebastopol Flat, the Chinese are our neighbours. I grew up around them, I can speak some of their language. I prefer some of them to most of the whites I know."

Ned leans in.

"Sebastopol is near El Dorado, isn't it?"

"Aye."

"I don't suppose you know Senior-constable Hall?"

"Only by repute. His character is well known throughout the Woolshed," Joe says.

Ned pushes his hair back to reveal a collection of scars.

"The fat bastard beat me over the head with his six chambered colt revolver at Greta a few years ago. I'd love to repay his kindness."

"A credit to the force," Joe scoffs, "no better than that bloody snob, Mullane. Right, Aaron?"

Aaron smirks.

"Takes a rogue to catch a rogue."

Ned laughs and claps a hand on Aaron's back.

"There are no better thieves in the country than the police. I had three years' experience in Beechworth and Pentridge. When I went in, I had over thirty head of the very best horses the land could produce, but when I got my liberty, I could only find one."

Joe and Aaron give Ned their full attention.

"That scoundrel Constable Flood stole them, and then sold most to the navvies on the railway line. He is the greatest horse stealer about and while he wears the jacket, he is free to carry on the same game."

Joe shakes his head in disgust.

"Yet, we are expected to abide their laws without question."

"There is no justice in the English laws lads, but any amount of injustice to be had," Ned retorts, picking up his cabbage tree hat from the bar and positions it on his head, a red fly veil tied around its crown. "Danny and I need to be heading home, but if you're ever in Greta ask after us and we'll go and get a drink at O'Brien's?"

"We're back in court tomorrow," Joe says mournfully, "but if they allow us our freedom, I'll be there."

Ned clasps Joe's hand firmly.

"We'll be seeing you."

He shakes Aaron's hand and they leave.

Aaron turns to Joe.

"I thought he was going to blow your head off when you mentioned the bushranging."

XII

After a night spent in one of the Albion Hotel's advertised "spacious, lofty, and well-ventilated bedrooms," Joe and Aaron are again arranged behind the dock of the Beechworth Courthouse on the charge of maliciously wounding.

It had been a long night for Joe, knowing that a verdict would finally be reached. *Will I be discharged, fined, or sentenced?* His mind flitters uneasily between the three outcomes, and with no promised answer to soothe him he had tossed and turned anxiously. Seeing Ah On crouched in the dirt, his head bloodied, crying out for his mates, seemed like a distant memory, but the consequences were still fettered around his ankles. *I'm honest these days*, Joe reflected on Ned Kelly's words, a way of life he himself had almost forgotten.

***

Standing in the dock, the pair, who the Crown Prosecutor declares, "belong to the class of rural larrikins," are again indicted for 'wilfully and maliciously assaulting a Chinaman.'

Dr. Fox, who has been treating Ah On in the Ovens District Hospital begins the evidence for the prosecution, stating that the man had been seriously injured and though the injury may heal up in time, it is permanent.

All for a bathe in that bloody dam, Joe reflects as Ah On is helped into the box to give evidence for the final time. His cheek and temple are still stained with dark bruising, and the stitches concealing where the shattered bone has been removed are crusty with blood, giving the appearance of having recently opened back up.

With the evidence from the prosecution and the defence being almost identical to what had been given previously, Joe's attention shifts to the journalist for the *Ovens and Murray Advertiser*. They sit pencilling shorthand into a notebook as the proceedings progress. Joe is mesmerised by the man's ability to write without looking down at his paper, the noise of the courtroom blurring into the background, until a burst of laughter from Aaron breaks his trance.

Joe looks over at the witness box where Aaron's brother Willie stands.

"Both the prisoners were bleeding on the arms from the blows the Chinamen gave them with the bamboos. Ah On was hammering the defendant all the time he was running," he says gesturing a hammering motion with his fist.

Joe thumps Aaron's knee, the action concealed by the dock from the journalist who now fixes his glance in their direction.

"Shut up, you fool," Joe whispers.

Aaron winks at the journalist who shakes his head and mutters under his breath.

After his sister Mary gives her testimony, repeating word for word what she had been taught by Joe and Aaron, the court is adjourned, with the evidence now to be deliberated by the men of the Jury. Joe and Aaron are led back down the narrow hall and into the male holding cell.

The Jury deliberates for two and a half hours, during which time Joe paces along the length of the small cell, feeling certain that Aaron's show in the courtroom will have unravelled any hope at leniency they may have had.

At twenty past two, the pair are called back in for sentencing. Joe holds his breath, his knuckles turning white as he grips onto the railing of the dock as Judge Hackett is passed the piece of paper that contains the verdict of the Jury.

"Joseph Byrne," the Judge begins, his deep voice filling the room, "this court finds you not guilty. Aaron Sherritt, you are found guilty of a common assault, committed in self-defence. Discharge prisoner Byrne."

Not guilty. Joe closes his eyes; two months of uncertainty and unease dissipating with the thud of the Judge's gavel.

"The verdict for my client, Aaron Sherritt, is virtually one of not guilty, is it not?" Mr. Brown protests.

The Judge considers his question before turning back to address the Bench.

"I am sorry to inconvenience the Jury, but I must ask for at least a reasonable verdict."

Let the bastard sweat a little, Joe muses as the colour drains from his mate's face.

***

From the courthouse, Joe is led across to the police station to sign the papers for his discharge. Entering the station, he is greeted by a constable whose cheeks are marred by a collection of pockmarks.

As Joe passes the signed documents back across, a familiar voice fills the room.

"Told you I'd get off."

Joe rolls his eyes and turns around to face Aaron.

"You were lucky."

Aaron leans his elbows on the bench to sign his papers.

"I had a *very narrow escape*," he says, imitating the gravelly voice of the Judge, "throwing stones is a low and blackguard practise, apparently."

The constable retrieves Aaron's signed papers with a look of disapproval.

***

Retrieving their horses, they lead them out of the paddock and prepare to mount.

"Heading home?" Aaron asks, vaulting into the saddle.

"No, I think I'll head over to Greta."

Aaron looks at Joe sceptically.

"They invited you too," Joe adds as a way of appeasement.

Aaron thinks for a moment.

"I better tag along to make sure you don't get into trouble. I wouldn't want to be around your ma when she finds out you've been drinking with a bushranger fresh out of court."

"It's alright," says Joe, "maybe Ned's honesty will rub off on us?"

Acknowledgements

The writing of this book would not have been possible without the love, support and inspiration I am given from a number of people, and I would like to thank them here.

Firstly, I wish to acknowledge the love and support I am shown by my darling husband, Aidan Phelan. He has been the biggest supporter of my work since my days of sharing small snippets of it on Facebook, back in 2017, and has continued to instil in me the confidence to keep going, even when I falter. Aidan is also my illustrator and editor, and I am extremely grateful to be able to include his beautiful pieces alongside my writing. I should also point out that he is the driver on our many trips to Kelly Country, and never once grumbles, not out loud anyway, about having to stop into Benalla Cemetery, so that I may say hello, and goodbye, to Joe. For that, I am very appreciative.

Secondly, to Joe and Aaron, who continue to inspire me, as well as granting me a sense of purpose in researching and telling their stories, for I would not be who I am without their constant presence within my life. Joe, especially, shapes so much of what I do, and indeed who I am, and his story has given me an abundance of strength, direction, and courage when I have needed it the most.

Thirdly, to my family, who continue to show me support and love, even though they may have not always understood my passion, and because I promised my brother I would include it, YES AFL TEAM/YES STADIUM. (My Tasmanian readers will understand.)

To Jesse Sanderson from *Kellyland Glenrowan*, who not only supports and stocks my books, but who has also become a friend, and Noeleen Lloyd, another cherished friend who continues to support and inspire me.

And finally, my loyal readers, with a special thank you to friend and supporter, Airi Repetti, who has been with me since I first began *An Outlaw's Journal* in July 2018. I am so very grateful for the support I receive from each and every one of you, whether it be through interactions on social media or the purchasing and reading of my books.

You all give me the courage and determination to keep writing and researching Joe's story, and I am so grateful for that.

- Georgina Phelan (née Stones), 2023.

An Outlaw's Journal

Behind the Journal

The incident at the dam on the 13th of January 1877 has always interested me and is one that has raised many questions. Not merely because of the way it escalated so rapidly, but because of the simmering tension that *may* have sparked it.

According to Ah On, Joe had previously thrown rocks at his hut, so why was this? Especially when Joe was on friendly terms with many of the Chinese, and would later come to save the life of a Chinese acquaintance during his outlawry. Was it simply due to Ah On's supposed ownership of the dam? As can be interpreted through Joe's action of calling on the man to see him bathing and Margaret's statement of it being ownerless, or did it run deeper?

Ian Jones states in *The Fatal Friendship* that Ah Seong, one of the men who shared a hut with Ah On, was called a "black Chinaman" by the other Chinese. This may help explain why the three men were separated from the main Chinese camp. Perhaps all three men were equally as distrusted by their countrymen, but for what reason? For the narrative of *Blood and Bamboo* I have used the brutal fight that occurred between a man named Ah Fook and another named Ah On in 1874, to help explain why he *may* have been so mistrusted and disliked. Of course, there is no indisputable evidence tying the Ah On who lived near the Byrnes with the one who had badly injured Ah Fook, but it is an interesting idea to ponder.

Another crucial detail I wished to explore was Joe's own statement of *"the bastard will never put me away again,"* when looking at the dying and bleeding body of his once-best-friend. According to one of the police hiding in Aaron's hut on the night of his murder on the 26th of June 1880, Aaron had been jovially retelling the story of their arrest for the wounding of Ah On. Had Joe overheard this conversation while he waited outside the hut? Was it this final bluster from Aaron that made him utter those words so coldly? Ah On could have easily been killed by the rock Aaron had thrown, which would have seen both young men charged with murder, and for a time his condition was gravely serious. How would this uncertainty have made Joe feel, especially when coupled with Aaron's inability to take things seriously? Given Joe had only recently been released after his six-month sentence for the butchering of the El Dorado School cow, how would he have felt at the possibility of being sent back behind those oppressive granite walls? He *may* have experienced feelings of anxiety, anger, fear, and guilt, which are all emotions I wanted to portray within the narrative, as I felt it important to highlight how the incident *may* have affected Joe and why those final words to Aaron were so powerful.

In conjunction with the incident with Ah On and the particulars surrounding it, other events I wished to explore which occurred between November 1876 and March 1877, was Joe's release from Beechworth Gaol; the birth of his former sweetheart Ellen Byron's first baby, which had been conceived before her marriage to Martin Byron; Aaron's arrest for cruelty to a horse; and their meeting with Dan Kelly while waiting in the Beechworth lockup. These incidents help to add further context as to what else was happening in Joe's life at that time, which is why I felt them important to include within the narrative.

Also, as Joe spoke and understood Cantonese, I felt it integral to include phrases and words in this language, which I have endeavoured to highlight within the narrative as much as I can. This was included, also, as a way of capturing realism and to show respect to the spoken language of the Chinese miners, cooks and storekeepers who had emigrated from Hong Kong. The internet site, Omniglot, has proven imperative in this understanding and can be sourced at: https://omniglot.com/language/phrases/cantonese.php.

While I acknowledge some of the historical language used throughout the book is offensive when viewed from a 2023 perspective, I believed it important to use it in the narrative to appropriately show the language used within the context of the events, as well as the attitudes behind the use of such language in late-1800's Australia.

Finally, I hope that in reading the narrative and the following pages of historical context, it enables for a deeper understanding of what occurred and how the choices Joe and Aaron made affected them and those around them.

Murderous Assault

The following snippet appeared in the *Ovens and Murray Advertiser* three days after the fight at the dam and, if it was read by Joe or Aaron, or relayed to them, would have been their first glimpse at the seriousness of Ah On's condition.

It is worth noting that only Aaron is named as the attacker, although this would have been unlikely to have given Joe peace of mind.

'Yesterday, a Chinaman named Ah Hong (Ah On), a miner residing at Sebastopol, was admitted into the Ovens District Hospital, suffering from a dangerous wound in the face. Upon examination, Dr Farr found that the zygomatic arch, or what scientific men would call the cheekbone, was broken into five pieces. The wound is a horrible one, and the patient lies in a dangerous state. From what we can learn, the wound was inflicted by a stone thrown at the Chinaman, who bears the character of being a harmless fellow, by Mr Aaron Sherritt, of Sheep Station Creek. We have not heard full particulars, but from what we can learn, the assault was a most unprovoked and murderous one.'

OVENS AND MURRAY ADVERTISER, 16TH JANUARY, 1877, P.2.

Charged

The following are the details regarding the charges laid against Joe and Aaron, as published at the time, which I referred to when piecing together the events related in the narrative.

'On Tuesday Aaron Sherritt was charged before Mr W. Ward, J.P., with assaulting a Chinaman at Reid's Creek, and was remanded until the 13th inst.'

OVENS AND MURRAY ADVERTISER, 8TH FEBRUARY, 1877, P.3.

'On Wednesday, before Mr F. Brown, J.P., Joseph Byrnes was charged on warrant with inflicting grievous bodily harm on one Ah On at Sebastopol, by throwing stones and striking him on the head, and was remanded until Tuesday.'

OVENS AND MURRAY ADVERTISER, 8TH FEBRUARY, 1877, P.2.

Petty Sessions Trial

The following is the reporting of the Petty Sessions Trial as it appeared in the *Ovens and Murray Advertiser*. It is important to note that this may have been the first time Joe and Aaron had seen Ah On since the altercation, with the wounded man still a patient at the hospital, and, if nothing else, would have highlighted the gravity of the situation.

It is also clear from the evidence of Margaret and Anne that they did not see the rock thrown by Aaron, and so, connecting the thrown stick and Ah On falling down, despite it going past him and falling into the race, they assumed this had caused him to fall.

GRIEVOUS ASSAULT. Aaron Sherritt and Joseph Byrne were charged with assaulting one Ah On at the Woolshed, with intent to do grievous bodily harm. Mr F. Brown appeared for Sherritt, and Mr Zincke for Byrne.

Ah On, the complainant, deposed that he was a miner, residing at Sebastopol, where he had lived several years. His mates (Ah Seong and Ah Sing) lived in the same hut. There was a dam 60 or 80 yards from the hut, and a garden between them. He was in the garden on the evening of the 13th January, when he saw the defendant Byrne bathing in the dam; Sherritt was on the dam, but not undressed. They called out to witness. Witness then went with Ah Seong, and they were engaged washing their feet just outside the hut, when both prisoners threw stones at them. He knew Sherritt about 10 months, and Byrne over two years. Sherritt threw a stone at him, but it did not strike him. Witness walked away to his hut, where his mates were. The defendants came up and threw stones at them. Sherritt threw the first stone, but that look no effect; the other prisoner also threw a stone without any effect. Sherritt then threw another stone, which struck witness near the right temple, and caused the injury he still had. Witness called out, and his mate Ah Seong took up a stick and ran after Byrne, and witness ran after Sherritt in the direction of Mrs. Byrnes house, about 80 or 90 yards. Witness then felt giddy and sat down, the wound being bleeding. His mates then came up, and they helped him back to his hut. He came to Beechworth the following day, and saw Dr Fox, and went to the hospital the same evening, where he was still a patient. Had not seen the defendants previous to the assault on the same day. There was only the one blow caused by the stone as described.

By Mr Brown: Nothing else occurred at the dam before the stone-throwing. Byrne called out to him to have a look at them bathing. I took a stick to chase them after I was struck with the stone. I did not strike Sherritt with the stick, and never got within five or six yards of him. Sherritt picked up the stick, and threw it at me, but it fell into a race. Did not see Mrs Byrne nor little Mary Byrne.

By Mr Zincke: The defendants were dressed. My mate did not catch Byrne. Sherritt threw the stone that struck me. Ah Seong, mate of last witness, corroborated his evidence in every particular. Witness picked up the stone when he came back that struck his mate. There was blood on it. He handed the stone to Constable Mullane. The stone produced was the same (a rugged piece of rock, the size of a small list). Nothing was adduced in cross-examination.

Ah Sing, another mate of prosecutor's, proved that stones were thrown, but as he was inside the hut cooking, he could not see who threw the stones. He then saw his mates with their bamboos chasing the defendants.

Dr Fox stated that on the 14th January last Ah On, the prosecutor, came to him. He had two wounds on the right side of his face, one larger and deeper than the other, and about ¾ of an inch from his ear. This communicated with a broken hone. The other wound was about an inch from the first, and was more superficial. Both these wounds were over the zygomatic arch, composed of bone. Subsequently at the hospital assisted Dr Farr in removing five pieces of bone from the man's face. These pieces were connected with the wounds described. Prosecutor was still a patient at the hospital. Witness regarded the wounds at one time as dangerous. There was permanent injury done to the prosecutor. He would not be able to masticate as well, and the wound would, no doubt produce disfigurement. The stone produced, thrown with considerable violence, would have produced the injuries. The projections on the stone on the side which, the blood is would have exactly produced the wounds.

By Mr Brown: Believe the marks on the stone to be blood, but could not answer definitely without microscopical examination. A man with such a wound might run 40 or 50 yards. Would rather have expected him to have sat down immediately on receiving the blow.

Mounted-constable Mullane deposed that he went to the hut of prosecutor at Sebastopol on the 15th January, and was handed the stone produced by the witness Ah Seong. It is in the same state now. On the 15th arrested the prisoner Byrne at Sheepstation Creek on a warrant. Told him the charge, and cautioned him, and asked him if he had anything to say. He said, "I have nothing to say; I did not do it, and I did not see it done." I said, "Were you and Sherritt together at Sebastopol on the 13th January?" He said, " I don't know if it was the 13th, but we were there the day the Chinaman got hurt." I said if so, it was strange that he knew nothing about the assault. He said it happened in this way — "We were bathing in the dam; when we got out the Chinamen hunted us with bamboos; I ran one way, and Aaron ran the other, and I saw nothing at all of it."

Mounted-constable McCracken, stationed at El Dorado, deposed that he arrested prisoner Sherritt on the morning of the 5th about 5 miles from El Dorado, towards Chiltern, on the warrant produced. Told him the charge, and cautioned him. He said, "I admit the charge; he ran after me and struck me first, and I then struck him with a stick."

There was no mention made of the other prisoner by either prisoner or witness. This closed the case for the prosecution.

For the defence, Margaret Byrne, mother of prisoner Byrne, residing at Sebastopol close to the dam, remembered the evening the Chinaman was hurt. Saw the Chinaman running after Sherritt with a bamboo, and hit him a couple of times. Sherritt picked up a stick and threw it at the Chinaman. It struck the Chinaman on the side of the head and knocked him down.

By Sergeant Baber: Could not say what side of the head the Chinaman was struck. They were about 37 feet from where I was, which was about 50 yards from the Chinaman's hut. It was Ah On that was struck.

To Mr Brown: Mrs Sherritt and my children were there. The other Chinaman chased my son for about 200 yards, and then went back. The Chinaman was calling out for Ah On, and picked up Ah On's slick. The Chinaman that ran after my son picked up Ah On's stick and the stick Sherritt threw at Ah On, besides his own.

Anne Sherritt, mother of the boy Aaron Sherritt, was at Mrs Byrne's the day the Chinaman was hurt, and corroborated the previous witness' evidence as to how the case occurred. There is blood at the place the Chinaman was struck, on the bridge, still.

By Sergeant Baber: Believe the Chinaman was struck on the right side of the head.

William Sherritt, a boy of about 13 years, son of

last witness, swore that the assault was commenced by the Chinamen at the dam, and that the defendants ran away with the Chinamen after them, and otherwise confirmed his mother's evidence verbatim.

By Sergeant Baber: I heard the witnesses ordered out of court this morning. I was in court just now, while my mother and Mrs Byrne's gave evidence.

His Worship said he could not now refuse to take the evidence, but it would not be worth very much.

Mary Byrne, a child, who stated she was 12 years of age, and brother of the prisoner Byrne, corroborated the other witnesses for the defence.

The prisoners, who said nothing, were committed for trial at the next Court of General Sessions, to be held at Beechworth on Wednesday, 28th February. Bail allowed to each in their own surety of £50 and two sureties of £25 each. The court then adjourned.

OVENS AND MURRAY ADVERTISER, 15TH FEBRUARY, 1877, P.3

Bail Secured

Despite the large amount required, £75 each, the two families managed to scrape together enough money to secure bail for Joe and Aaron. Given their inability to pay bail the previous year for the butchering of the cow, it shows the Byrnes and Sherritts saw reason to support the pair. It may have been because, unlike the case with the cow, it was not so clear cut, and perhaps Ah On's previous actions surrounding ownership of the dam had made Margaret and other Sebastopol residents, if she had sought help from them, determined to make a stand. It is supposition, of course, as we will never know how or why two impoverished families were able to come up with such a large sum of money at such short notice for this case and not others.

On Bail.

Aaron Sherritt and Joseph Byrne, maliciously wounding, Beechworth.

OVENS AND MURRAY ADVERTISER, 17TH FEBRUARY, 1877, P.5

General Sessions Trial

The following is the reporting of the General Sessions Trial as it appeared within the *Ovens and Murray Advertiser*. The evidence is virtually the same as it was during the Petty Sessions, apart from the addition of certain details, such as William Sherritt's over-embellishment of what happened, which prompted a laugh from Aaron, and Margaret Byrne's exaggeration of the size of the stick Aaron had thrown, describing it as if it was a small log.

When reading the evidence, while understandable that Joe would be discharged, it is a miracle Aaron was also, as drilled into him by Judge Hackett.

Unlawfully wounding. Aaron Sherritt and Joseph Byrne answered to their bail on the charge of unlawfully wounding Ah On, and pleaded not guilty. Prisoners were defended by Messrs F. Brown and Zincke.

His Honor, in face of an application for an adjournment, decided to have the prisoners arraigned and the jury sworn in, and then the following jurors having been sworn, the Judge discharged the other jurors from further attendance: — Martin May, (foreman), Thos. Sandham, Ogilvie Stewart, Daniel T. Pye, William Mason, Robert Wetherow, Nicholas Sauverin, Richard Kain, George Cross, William Glover, George Wright, and Edward Keogh. The Court subsequently adjourned till this Thursday morning, at ten o'clock.

OVENS AND MURRAY ADVERTISER, 1ST MARCH, 1877, P.3.

Maliciously Wounding. Aaron Sherritt and Joseph Byrne again surrendered to their bail on a charge of maliciously wounding. Mr Brown appeared for both prisoners — for Sherritt instructed by Mr Zincke.

The jury sworn on the previous evening were again called as follows: — Martin May, (foreman), Thos. Sandham, Ogilvie Stewart, Daniel T. Pye, William Mason, Robert Wetherow, Nicholas Sauverin, Richard Kain, George Cross, William Glover, George Wright, and Edward Keogh.

The evidence was for the most- part a mere repetition of that taken at the police court inquiry, but the case appears so important that we repeat it in full.

Dr Fox stated that he had examined the prosecutor on the 14th January. He had two wounds on the right side of the face, one of which communicated with a broken bone. This was the larger and deeper wound of the two. He was seriously injured. The risk was so great that witness ordered him to the Hospital, and assisted in an operation there, when there were five pieces of bone removed from the zygomatic arch. A stone like that produced would have caused the wound. There were two projections on the stone which exactly corresponded with the two wounds, and the stone would have produced the wounds if thrown about the length of the court with great violence. A Chinese bamboo could not have produced the wounds. The injury was permanent; it might heal up in time, but the bone was still unsound.

By Mr Brown: You can imagine a piece of hard wood producing these wounds, and I would have expected the man to fall immediately on receiving such a crushing blow, but I cannot imagine it with this stone before me.

Ah On, the prosecutor, a miner, said he resided at Sebastopol, and had done so about ten years. There were two other Chinamen residing with him, Ah Seong and Ah Sin. On Saturday, 14th January he returned to his hut at half-past 6 o'clock in the evening. There is a dam about 50 yards from the hut with a garden between. He went there to water his vegetables, and saw "Joe" (speaking of Byrne) bathing in the dam. The other prisoner, Sherritt, was on the bank. Had known "Joe" over 10 years, and Sherritt a few months. "Joe" called him to look at him in the water, and Sherritt threw a stone at him. Took no notice of that, but went back to the hut. Ah Seong was changing his clothes outside. Ah Sin was inside cooking. Witness and Ah Seong were outside washing their feet, when they saw prisoners again about 25 yards from the hut. Sherritt threw a stone at them first, and then Byrne threw one. These stones struck the hut, but not the witness or his mate. Sherritt then threw a second stone which struck him on the side of the face. (The wound was near the temple.) Witness called Ah Seong to get a stick and run after the prisoners. Witness ran after Sherritt, and Ah Seong after Joe. Sherritt ran towards Joe's house, and witness followed him about 60 or 70 yards from the hut, but could not get up to him. He then got giddy and crouched down. He was not nearer than six or seven yards to Sherritt at any time. The stick witness had was one the Chinese carry weights on. It was about a yard and a half long, and smooth. He did not strike Sherritt with that stick. His mates then brought him to the hut. He did not strike Sherritt at all during this time. He had given Sherritt no provocation. Had called him no names nor said anything to him nor to the other prisoner.

By Mr Brown: Had no dispute with Byrne before this, but Byrne had several times thrown stones at the house. I took the stick to try to hit Sherritt after he hit me with the stone. Before I sat down Sherritt threw a stick at me, but it did not hit me. I then sat down. I said nothing while I was running after Sherritt. Ah Seong ran after Byrne in a different direction. I remained sitting down till my mates came to me and picked me up. I saw nothing of Mrs Sherritt or Mrs Byrne. It was near Mrs Byrne's garden. Mrs Byrne's door is 40 or 50 yards from where I sat down.

To the Crown Prosecutor: The stick Sherritt threw at me did not hit me; it was a light kind of stick. Ah Seong, a miner, and mate of last witness, corroborated his evidence in every particular, except that he did not see Sherritt throw the stick last spoken of, as he was running after Byrne at that time. He, however, swore positively that he saw Sherritt throw the stone which inflicted the wound on the prosecutor. The witness did not catch up to Joe nor hit him. When witness looked round his mate was sitting on the ground, and bleeding from the temple. It was Sherritt who threw the stone that inflicted that injury. He saw the stone that struck his mate, and picked it up. When his mate was struck he cried out, "I am hurt." He picked up the stone before running after Joe. He handed the stone to Constable Mullane. He first picked up the stone produced, when it struck his mate, and put it to one side. He then picked it up again, when he brought back his mate, and took it into his hut. Neither he nor prosecutor gave either of the prisoners any provocation whatever.

By Mr Brown: The stone is in the same state now as when he picked it up. The stains were on it then the same as now.

Ah Sin, mate of prosecutor and last witness, saw a stone thrown, but he was inside cooking when his mate was struck. He went to Ah On, who was bleeding, and wounded. Witness and Ah Seong helped Ah On back to the hut.

By Mr Brown: He was inside in the kitchen part at the time, and sometimes outside. When they took Ah

On back to the hut they had two sticks with them and no others.

Mounted-constable Mullane had gone to Sebastopol on the 15th January. Got the stone produced from Ah Seong. There seemed to be something like marks of blood on it then, somewhat plainer than they are now. Arrested Byrne on the 6th February at Sheep Station Creek and cautioned him. Asked him if he had anything to say in answer to the charge. He said "I have nothing to say; I did not do it or see it done." I asked him if he were at Sebastopol on the 13th January. He said "I don't- know if it was the 13th, but I was there the day the Chinaman got hurt." On the way to the lock-up I said to him "it is strange if you were there you know nothing of the assault." He said "it occurred in this way, we were bathing in the dam and the Chinaman ran after us; Aaron ran one way and I the other."

Mounted-constable McCracken, stationed at El Dorado, arrested prisoner Sherritt on the 5th of February in the ranges about 4 miles from El Dorado in the direction of Chiltern. Told him the charge. He said "I admit the charge; I assaulted the Chinaman, but be struck me first."

By Mr Brown: I think he did say the Chinaman ran after him. He was stripping bark when I arrested him.

This closed the case for the Crown, and Mr Brown, after addressing the jury, called the following evidence:

Margaret Byrne, mother of prisoner Byrne, resided at Sebastopol, close on 100 yards from the Chinese dam. On the evening the Chinaman was hurt was at her own place. Heard the Chinese sing out. Looked out, and saw the prosecutor run after Sherritt with a bamboo. Sherritt picked up a stick, and ran as far as the bridge. He then slewed round, and flung his stick at the Chinaman. It struck him on the side of the head, and the Chinaman fell down. The Chinaman had struck Sherritt twice before this.

By the Crown Prosecutor: The dam does not belong to anyone. The Chinaman struck Sherritt with the stick twice on the back. He did not knock him down. The stick Sherritt picked up was about two yards long, and as thick as your leg. Saw blood on the Chinaman's face when he fell, but not when he was running. I was standing on the verandah, and they were running towards me. The Chinaman was struck on the right side of the head. Sherritt was about a yard or two from the Chinaman when he struck him. Mrs Sherritt was there.

Anne Sherritt, mother of prisoner, deposed: Sherritt was present on the occasion of the assault. This witness corroborated last witness' evidence. She added that the Chinaman that came up to prosecutor took the stick with him that his mate had been struck with. The Chinaman struck her son two or three times before he threw the stick. (Witness' depositions were here read, in which she said that the Chinaman was "striking at" her son.)

William Sherritt, son of last witness, also corroborated the evidence for the defence, and stated that in the first instance the prisoners were bathing in the dam, when Ah On came out and ordered them out of the dam. The two Chinamen then came out with sticks and ran after prisoners. There was no blood on the Chinaman's face till he fell.

By Mr Armstrong: Both the prisoners were bleeding on the arms from the blows the Chinamen gave them with the bamboos. Ah On was hammering my brother all the time he was running after him. The stick my brother threw at the Chinaman was about as thick as your wrist. (He pointed to a piece of wood in court to show its thickness.)

Mary Byrne, a child of 12 years of age, told the same story as young Sherritt, and repeated it word for word twice to the Crown Prosecutor, just as if she had learned it as a lesson.

The jury retired at 10 minutes past 12, and returned into court at 20 minutes past 2 o'clock with the following extraordinary verdict: "Joseph Byrne, Not

Guilty; Aaron Sherritt, 'Guilty of a common assault, committed in self-defence.' "

Byrne was accordingly discharged and Mr Brown pointed out that the finding against Sherritt was virtually one of Not Guilty. His Honor said he was sorry to inconvenience the jury, but he must ask for at least a reasonable verdict. The jury, having again retired for a few minutes, returned with a verdict of Not Guilty. His Honor, in discharging the prisoner, warned him that he had a very narrow escape, and cautioned him against throwing stones again as it was a low and blackguard practice.

OVENS AND MURRAY ADVERTISER, 3RD MARCH, 1877, P.1

Better Known to the Police than to the Schoolmaster

The journalist for the *Ovens and Murray Advertiser* was not impressed by the 'two larrikins' he observed standing in the dock, as highlighted within the following report he made in that publication. That he compares the duo to local bushrangers Smith and Brady as a warning is somewhat prophetic.

On Thursday two youths, better known to the police than to the schoolmaster, and who, as the Crown Prosecutor put it, belonged to the class of rural larrikins, were indicted for wilfully and maliciously assaulting a Chinaman. According to the story of three Chinamen, whose testimony bore internal evidence of truth, the assault was unprovoked. Moreover, it was sworn by Dr Fox that the stone produced by the Chinaman as having been that with which the two contiguous wounds were inflicted on the prosecutor's head, near the temple, would, if thrown with sufficient force, have exactly caused the injuries actually inflicted; and that in fact, with that stone before you, you would have to go into the realms of imagination to picture a stick which would have produced the same effect. For, the theory of the defence was that the injury had been inflicted by a stick thrown at the prosecutor while he was in the unprovoked pursuit of the prisoner Sherritt. The evidence for the defence was that of the mothers of the defendants, a young brother of one of them (whose demeanour was sufficiently suggestive of our someday seeing him in his brother's place), and the sister of the other, an intelligent looking little girl of 12 years of age, who it was painful to hear repeating the story twice over to the Crown Prosecutor which she already told to Mr Brown for the prisoners, just as if she were repeating a lesson - which there is no doubt she was. We have no hesitation in saying that the testimony of the Chinaman was in no way to be impugned, and to get over Dr Fox's evidence was impossible, unless a man, with a plain fact before him, goes out of his way to find some almost impossible solution. On the other hand, the defence was utterly improbable on the face of it - first, because Chinamen are not in the habit of pursuing and assaulting Europeans without provocation, but simply for amusement, as our larrikins are in the habit of treating them; next, there were some glaring discrepancies in the evidence; for instance, Mrs Byrne swore that the stick thrown by Sherritt was six feet long, and as thick as the Crown Prosecutor's leg - meaning his thigh, which was the only part of his leg then visible to the witness - while the boy Sherritt explained it being about as thick as the lower ring of the barristers' form, which was not larger than a man's wrist, and last there were totally new elements introduced, such as the wounds inflicted by the Chinaman on the prisoners. The description of those injuries made the prisoner Sherritt himself laugh, to think that he should have been so terribly wounded and still live to be tried by his country - and as it turned out to be, acquitted by that country's representatives. There is undoubtedly a ludicrous side to a trial which results in a verdict "guilty of an assault committed in self-defence," but there is also a very serious aspect to this particular case, owing to the character, the career, and the proclivities of the defendants. We would just remind these two strapping lads of the fate of Smith and Brady, who commenced life like them, and ended it on the gallows.

OVENS AND MURRAY ADVERTISER, 3RD MARCH, 1877, P.1.

The Bastard Will Never Put Me Away Again

The following is said to have come from one of the four constables that hid in Aaron's hut on the night he was murdered by Joe on 26 June 1880. It offers a key insight into the way Aaron viewed the Ah On incident and, of course, he positions himself as the voice of reason. This is partly why I have characterised Aaron as being far more flippant regarding the trouble he and Joe got into over the assault, and is just one of many examples of such an attitude from Aaron towards his reckless and criminal behaviours.

A singular story is told by one of the constables who was present in Sherritt's hut on the night of Sherritt's murder. He states that a conversation was being carried on between Sherritt, Mrs. Sherritt, Mrs. Barry, and himself, and that the subject of their remarks was Joe Byrne. Sherritt then proceeded to tell a yarn about Byrne and himself having once been arrested on a serious charge. He said they assaulted a Chinaman and nearly killed him. The Celestial indeed was so near death's door that he had to be fed with a silver tube. He himself was arrested sometime after, but Byrne succeeded in evading the police. Whilst he was lying in the Beechworth lockup one night, he heard someone knocking outside, and on asking who it was, heard Joe Byrne reply. "It is me; I am going to help you to escape." Sherritt said he replied, "The Chinaman is getting better, so you had better give your-self up, and do not be a fool." Byrne took his advice, surrendered, and secured legal assistance, and was acquitted. Just when Sherritt had finished this story a knock came to the door, and as is now well known, it proved to be the intimation of the final visit Sherritt was to receive from Joe Byrne.

THE ARGUS (MELBOURNE), 6TH AUGUST, 1880, P.6

It should be pointed out that Joe never evaded the police as the pair were arrested only a day apart and, as it was Aaron who threw the rock, it would have been he who the police most concerned themselves with. Furthermore, Joe was charged on warrant, and after Mullane had failed to find him at Sebastopol, he would have known Joe would likely be at Sheepstation Creek, either at the Sherritt selection or in Aaron's hut, which was exactly where he was found.

(For further reading regarding Joe's relationship with Aaron Sherritt, please refer to my previous books, *Ah Nam* and *Joe Byrne and The Cow from El Dorado*.)

The Incident at the Stockyard

The following report was made a few days after Joe's death. I have included it because it is often used as a means to suggest Joe was dangerous or unhinged.

Firstly, the identity of the witness to the event is unknown and the sister unnamed. It must also be acknowledged that none of Joe's sister's appearances were ever commented upon with having such a facial disfigurement caused by Joe's violence. During Joe's outlawry, several policemen were known to have visited the Byrne home and yet not one of them commented upon the appearance of the injured girl.

I have included it within the narrative to show that Joe did indeed have a temper and in a high-pressure situation, such as herding livestock, this anger may have presented itself, however, whether he acted in the same manner as described is arguable.

Byrne had a number of nicknames. He was the idol of the girls of the district, who said he was such a handsome, and such a mild young gentleman that no one would believe him to be capable of interfering with anybody. One anecdote will suffice to show how mild he was. Some time ago before he took to bush-ranging, he was running some horses to the stockyard at the Woolshed, The yard was old, and the fence was broken. He got his sister to help him, and to stand in one of the gaps in the fence. This is a time-honoured custom with the people of the district, who will go into a stockyard and chase the horses round them-selves, but they use the women to fill up the gaps in the fence. One of the horses was a very wild one, and this one Byrne wanted to catch. It rushed straight at his sister, and, knocking her aside, escaped from the yard. Byrne was foaming with rage; he rushed at his sister, seized her by the hair of the head with one hand, and struck her over the face with the heavy bridle he carried. He cut her face terribly, and knocked her eye out. So much for the ladies' man. He was called Sweet Birdie.

THE HERALD (MELBOURNE), 30TH JUNE, 1880, P.3.

A Sighting of Outlaw Joe by Ah On

The following report concerns Joe being spotted by Ah On while the Kelly Gang were preparing to head to Jerilderie in New South Wales in 1879, where they planned to rob the bank. Considering that the pair talked together, it is possible reconciliation had been made after the events by the dam, however, it obviously was not enough to halt Ah On going to the police to report the meeting.

It is now positively known that when the gang went to Jerilderie they started from the Buffalo Ranges, crossed the Little River near its source, then the Murray. A Chinaman who had been beaten with a stick by Joe Byrne previous to the outlawry met them on their way, recognised Byrne again, and talked with him, and subsequently reported his adventure to the police.

THE AUSTRALASIAN (MELBOURNE), 14TH AUGUST, 1880, P.1.

The Birth of a Son

While Joe was serving his six-month prison sentence, his old sweetheart, Ellen Byron, gave birth to her first son in October. Having married Martin Byron in July, this means the baby was conceived before the wedding, which would have brought a deal of scandal and may account for the marriage, which was evidently a deeply unhappy one for Ellen. It was also noted that a daughter born in 1878, appeared to be "half Chinese" and at the age of twelve had been deserted by Ellen. By 1890, Ellen and Martin had been separated for a "long time", with her now living with a man called James Watts.

77	16th October 1876 Chiltern Shire of Chiltern County of Bogong	James Martin not present	Male	Martin Byron, Herdsman 29 years County of Mayo Ireland	18th July 1876 Chiltern Victoria	Ellen Byron m.n. Salisbury 19 years Woolshed near Beechworth Victoria	21856.

Extract from the Chiltern register of births, 1876.
Source: Births, Deaths and Marriages Victoria.

(For further reading regarding Ellen Byron and her importance throughout Joe's life, both before and during his outlawry, please refer to my previous books *Ah Nam* and *Joe Byrne and the Cow from El Dorado*.)

Cruelty to a Horse

The following is a transcript of the trial for Aaron's charge of 'cruelty to a horse', as reported in the *Ovens and Murray Advertiser*. While there is no recorded evidence to suggest Joe accompanied Aaron into Beechworth with the loaded dray, I wanted to include it within the narrative for wider context, as well as to portray Joe's fears of going back to prison. Despite a grilling from Magistrate Pitcairn about the state of the horse, Aaron's father John failed to learn his lesson, and later that year his brother Jack would be arrested for cruelty to the same horse.

Before Mr R. Pitcairn, P.M., on Thursday last, Aaron Sherritt, on bail, appeared in answer to a charge of cruelly ill-using a horse. Mr F. Brown appeared for the defendant, and pleaded not guilty. The horse, which was outside the court, and was viewed by the police magistrate and likewise by our own reporter, was in a shocking state, both shoulders being completely stripped of skin to the flesh. The lining of the collar on each side was worn through, the straw stuffing appearing in holes corresponding with the holes in the unfortunate animal's shoulders, and dried blood on the collar showed what brutality had been exercised.

Sergeant Baber having stated the circumstances of the case, called Constable McHugh, who deposed that on Wednesday afternoon he saw the defendant in Beechworth, driving a dray with two horses and a load of hay; the defendant was endeavouring to urge the leader, but the animal appeared to have something wrong with him, and would not pull; there was a sack under the collar, and suspecting the reason of the horse avoiding the collar, witness examined him, and found the animal's shoulder as seen by the court; to prevent further cruelty he seized the lot and arrested the defendant.

Mr Brown thought the police might have allowed the man first to take his load of hay into Mr George Dennett's yards, where it was going, for by their action the hay was left exposed to the heavy rain, and although worth £4 it was now not worth 10s.

Sergeant Baber appealed to the bench as to whether they considered Constable McHugh had, in the slightest degree, exceeded his duty. When he seized the team, as he was empowered to do under the act, (the 23rd clause gives the police power under such circumstances to seize cart, load and all, and sell them if necessary in payment of any fine which might be inflicted), the defendant was still endeavouring to urge him on, and it was absolutely necessary to prevent further cruelty to seize the horse.

His Worship said that Constable McHugh had done perfectly right. He did not think, in all his experience, he had ever seen a more horrible case.

John Sherritt, father of the defendant, said he had sent his son in with the load of hay, and when he got into Beechworth himself he found his son in custody; the last-witness and Constable Mullane had taken the hay, horses and all, and the hay was now worth nothing; Mr Dennett would not take it.

By Sergeant Baber: One horse could not have taken the hay into Dennett's yard; did not try.

To the Bench: Did not ask Dennett if he would take the hay; could have hired a second horse to take it into the yard, but did not think of that. His Worship said this was the most disgraceful case he had ever met with in his life. If the father had been the driver instead of the son, he certainly would have sent him to gaol for three months. It was horrible to think of any one in human shape driving an unfortunate animal in such a condition, and it was no wonder the family bore the character it did when such practises were encouraged by the father himself. He ordered the defendant to pay a fine of £5 forthwith, the horse to be detained by the police and sold in satisfaction of the fine, unless it was paid, and in default of full satisfaction distress. The money was paid.

OVENS AND MURRAY ADVERTISER, 13TH JANUARY, 1877, P.4

A Curious Case of Saddle Stealing

The following report deals with Dan Kelly's charge of 'saddle stealing,' which saw him spend time in the Beechworth lockup with Joe and Aaron while he awaited trial. As yet, this is the earliest record we have for the three having met, although the scenes as depicted in the narrative are speculative.

In terms of a documented case of Aaron and Joe meeting the Kelly brothers for the first time, this is the closest we currently have. Further, this in combination with the narrow window of time between the Ah On case and the pair's involvement with Ned Kelly's horse stealing operation in 1877, indicates there was a good chance that this was actually the moment that set the ball rolling.

LARCENCY. Daniel Kelly was charged with stealing a saddle at Benalla, and pleaded not guilty. Mr F. Brown appeared for the defence. The following jury were sworn Robert Rae (foreman), John Carew, R. Douglass, Edward Keogh, J. Stephens, Christopher Kibble, Edwin Ansell, Geo. Cross, William Duncan, Henry Wiseman, Thomas Sutherland, and John Ewing.

Sidney Smith, a woolstaker, residing at Benalla, deposed that he had a saddle on the 4th of May last. Left it in the back kitchen of the Liverpool Arms about seven o'clock in the evening. Shut the door, and missed it the next morning. Identified the saddle produced by a seam which he had objected to on purchasing it, and by other marks.

Edward Shortell, a saddler at Benalla, deposed that he sold the saddle produced to prisoner over two years ago.

Mounted-constable Robinson deposed that he was at Benalla on the 30th of December, but was stationed at Richmond at present. Saw prisoner that day with the saddle produced. Asked him about the saddle. He first said he had bought it from one man, and afterwards from another.

By Mr F. Brown: It was five months from the time witness heard of the saddle being stolen until the arrest. Prisoner did not refuse to go with witness to see about the saddle. Prisoner gave two different accounts of how he came by the saddle. He produced a receipt subsequently at the police court.

This closed the case for the prosecution.

John Lloyd lived on the Kilfera Road, and knew the accused and was present at Eleven Mile Creek, where he dealt in a saddle with a man named Roberts. Prisoner gave Roberts a saddle and £1, and got another saddle in exchange. This happened at Skinner's (Skillion). Witness was one of the witnesses to the receipt produced.

By the Crown Prosecutor: Skinner (Skillion) was prisoner's brother-in-law. Witness was prisoner's cousin.

William Skinner (Skillion) knew the accused. Remembered a transaction about saddles at his house between the accused and Roberts, and they exchanged saddles, prisoner giving Roberts £1 to boot. Roberts wrote the receipt.

Edward Kelly, brother of the accused, knew Roberts, and had tried to find him for the purpose of this trial. Was present when the saddles were exchanged, and saw a receipt like the one produced, drawn out.

His Honor, in charging the jury, said he did not see why the prisoner was there at all. He had given a perfectly fair account of how he had come in to possession of the saddle, and the whole of the evidence corroborated that account. Verdict: Not Guilty. The accused was discharged.

OVENS AND MURRAY ADVERTISER, 1ST MARCH, 1877, P.2-3.

Dan Kelly
Public Domain

A Mysterious Death

NOTE: The following report is to be read with caution as it contains offensive language and possible references to self-harm.

This report details the finding of Ah Fook's body and while it is unknown who the specific "Ah On" was that fought with Ah Fook, for the purpose of the narrative and to help explain why Ah On was so mistrusted, I have surmised it to be him based on various context clues.

Unfortunately, given the way that these incidents were reported, which is to say that they were very light on details where the Chinese were concerned, we can only speculate on the links based on the various patterns we see in the way individuals with the same name were reported to have lived and behaved.

On Saturday afternoon the Beechworth police, in consequence of some information which had reached them, searched the neighbourhood of Wooragee for traces of a Chinaman who was supposed to have been missing for some days. On that evening they were unsuccessful, but next day they found the dead body of a Chinaman in the bush, nearly a mile from any habitation. It was in a frightful state of mutilation and decay. Some idea of its horrible condition can be gathered from such parts of the medical evidence given at the inquest (Ah Fook's scrotum had been cut off, he had slash wounds to the back of neck and both arms.) A more extraordinary ease, in many respects, we do not remember to have met with, and the evidence given at the inquest yesterday, renders the affair still more complicated. The story, so far as it was told by Ah Cheuy, was that the body was that of Ah Fook, who had been one of 17 partners, he, the witness, being one, in a mining at the Woolshed. The deceased lived with one Ah On, and same time since there was a quarrel between the two, when the witness saw Ah On knock Ah Fook down with a sapling. Ah On was bleeding from the head, too, and set out for the hospital, to which, as a matter of fact, he went, and remained several days. He returned to his hut on Sunday week, but the deceased had been missing for several days before this. The deceased had never been able to work after his quarrel with Ah On, but either laid in bed complaining, or crawled about, outside.

Then he was suddenly missed from his hut, and so far, as is at present shown, was never seen again until his corpse was discovered. Ah Cheuy, from whose evidence we mainly gather this fragment of a narrative, becoming anxious about Ah Fook, searched and inquired for him in all directions about the Woolshed, but discovering nothing, set off to Chiltern and the Indigo when he was aware that Ah Fook had friends. Nothing had been seen of him there, and Ah Cheuy returned to the Woolshed, whence on his arrival be immediately came in to Beechworth and telegraphed to Albury to make further inquiries, which were also entirely without result. On Friday, or early on Saturday, another Chinaman told him that a boy named William Fitzgerald had been saying that he had seen some clothes lying out in the bush. The two went to the boy and induced him to accompany them to the spot which he described, where they found some garments, similar to those worn by Chinamen, and stained with blood. This was not far from the Old Woolshed Police Camp. They went a few hundred yards further down the range, when they came upon the dead and mutilated body of Ah Fook. He was nearly naked, but several articles of clothing were lying beside or partly under him, and were in various places saturated with what seemed comparatively fresh blood. A pair of European boots were also beside the body. When we consider the circumstances of the case, so far as at present revealed, and more especially the extraordinary nature of the injuries inflicted, we are, we confess, utterly bewildered. There is, of course, the alternative possibility that Ah Fook, feeling himself helpless and infirm, killed himself by this cruel mode; but all the probabilities are against such a conclusion. The nature of the wounds is of so terrible a kind that it is hardly conceivable that any human being, however desirous of death, would inflict them upon himself. The medical evidence and opinions, too, are decidedly averse to his having been able to do so. The tendons and arteries of both wrists were severed, and the other injuries were so severe and so peculiar that we are come to the conclusion that a deliberate and revengeful crime has been committed. The finding of blood-stained clothes at some considerable distance from the body is another fact adding to the perplexity of the case. The anxiety shown throughout by Ah Cheuy is also rather a curious feature. The whole story reads more like one of those of the old Secret Societies, whose victims always bore special marks by which the initiated could recognise the authors, and so be deterred from offending against their laws, or like the torturing deaths inflicted by some tribes of Indians, each of which left as it were, its distinguishing signature of death upon those whom it slew. The inquest has been adjourned until Saturday next, and we trust in that time some fresh light may be thrown upon this strange occurrence. If the police have any clue, they very wisely keep it to themselves, but we know that no effort will be spared to discover and prove the truth, and as yet it must be remembered that there has been no time for wide and searching investigation.

OVENS AND MURRAY ADVERTISER, 5TH MAY, 1874, P.2.

The former Beechworth Methodist Church at the top of Ford Street. (c.1870s)
Author's Collection.

Beechworth looking towards the intersection of Loch and Camp Streets (c.1870s)
Author's collection.

Beechworth from the top of Ford Street looking towards the Beechworth Gaol.

Author's collection.

Beechworth Gaol [detail].

Author's collection.

Beechworth Courthouse.
Author's collection.

The remains of the police lock-up, Beechworth.
Author's collection.

'Swearing a Chinese Witness' from 'Our Chinamen'. The Australasian Sketcher, 21/02/1874.

Courtesy: State Library Victoria. 1654747; b49828.

Chinese on their way to the diggings, by Charles Lyall. (c.1854)
Courtesy: State Library Victoria. 1810211; wp001337.

[Detail]

Chinese sluicing, near Beechworth. [From a sketch by N. Chevalier, Esq]. Source: The Australian News for Home Readers, 25/08/1864.

Courtesy: State Library Victoria. 1688232; mp000785.

Chinese Encampment, by Charles Lyall. (c.1854)

Courtesy: State Library Victoria. 1810218; wp001342.

Chinese Costermonger. The Illustrated Australian News, 30/03/1868.

Courtesy: State Library Victoria. 1689795; mp001294.

These contemporary illustrations demonstrate the kind of bamboo that Ah On used to attack Aaron and Joe. These are very different from the ornamental bamboo rods people often use for interior decorating.

Reedy Creek
Author's collection.

The site of the Chinese gardens near El Dorado.

Author's collection.

Site of the Chinese gardens near El Dorado.
Author's collection.

[Detail]

A Chinese garden in Victoria, by J.C. Armytage. (c.1874-1876)

Courtesy: State Library Victoria. 2117147; is004047.

IN A CHINESE OPIUM DEN.—From a Flashlight Photo. by E. T. Luke.

In a Chinese opium den. (July 1896)

Courtesy: State Library Victoria. 1776348; mp008819.

Opium House, China, by John Henry Harvey.

Courtesy: State Library Victoria. 2150076; cf002736.

Notes

Prologue

- Ellen Salisbury being a sweetheart of Joe Byrne's. (*Royal Commission*, Q.13210, p.477.)
- Edward Kennedy's farm being abandoned and its location behind the Byrne selection. (*Ovens and Murray Advertiser*, 1 June, 1876.)
- Joe Byrne and Aaron Sherritt using Ned Kennedy's yard to brand stolen livestock. ((*Ovens and Murray Advertiser*, 1 June, 1876.)
- Joe Byrne having a scar on his left shin. (*Victoria Police Gazette* and Ian Jones, *The Fatal Friendship*, 2003, p.41.)
- The fight between Ah Nam and Robert Woods. (*Ovens and Murray Advertiser*, April 8, 1873.)
- Ellen Salisbury marrying Martin Byron. (*Ovens and Murray Advertiser*, 20 July, 1876.)
- Martin Byron being an alcoholic. (*Ovens and Murray Advertiser*, 3 June, 1893.)

Chapter 1

- Joe Byrne and Aaron Sherritt sentenced to 6 months in Beechworth Gaol with hard labour. (*Ovens and Murray Advertiser*, 1 June, 1876.)

Chapter 2

- The drought of 1876. (*Ovens and Murray Advertiser*, 4 August, 1876.)
- Joe Byrne being called 'Ah Joe.' (*Royal Commission*, q.14973, p.542.)

- Joe Byrne speaking Cantonese. (John Sadlier, *Recollections of a Victorian Policeman*, 1913, p.201.)
- Patrick Byrne's death on the 7th of November 1870. (*Ovens and Murray Advertiser*, 8 November, 1870.)
- 15-year-old Joe Byrne witnessing the torture of Ah Suey. (*Ovens and Murray Advertiser*, 10 May, 1872.)
- Joe Byrne borrowing Mrs. Batchelor knife and steel, and them failing to be returned to her. (*Ovens and Murray Advertiser*, 1 June, 1876.)
- Ellen Salisbury working for the Batchelors as Domestic Servant. (*The Herald* (Melbourne), 26 July, 1879.)
- The brawl between Ah Fook and Ah Oh. (*Ovens and Murray Advertiser*, 7 May, 1874.)
- Joe Byrne throwing rocks at Ah On's hut. (*Ovens and Murray Advertiser*, 3rd March, 1877.)
- Margret Byrne running a dairy. (*Ovens and Murray Advertiser*, July 29, 1879) and (Ian Jones, *The Fatal Friendship*, 2003, p.20)

Chapter 3

- Kate Byrne being friends with Ellen Salisbury. (*Ovens and Murray Advertiser*, 29 July, 1879.)
- Aaron Sherritt gifting Kate Byrne a bay filly. (*Ovens and Murray Advertiser*, 29 July, 1879.)
- The location of Martin Byron's hut. (*Benalla Standard*, 18 June, 1907.)
- Joe Byrne gifting his teenage sweetheart a lamb. (*Australian Son*, p.59.)
- Martin Byron herdsman for the Chiltern Common. (*Ovens and Murray Advertiser*, 21 July, 1873.)
- Ellen Salisbury being pregnant when she married Martin Byron, giving birth to a baby boy in October 1876 and calling him James Martin. (*Births, Deaths and Marriages Victoria.*)
- Martin Byron calling himself 'Lord Byron.' (*Royal Commission*, q.13858, p.503.) and (*Benalla Standard*, 18 June, 1907.)
- Martin Byron being an alcoholic. (*Ovens and Murray Advertiser*, 3 June, 1893.)
- Martin Byron having enemies. (*Ovens and Murray Advertiser*, 15 April, 1876), (*Ovens and Murray Advertiser*, 12 October, 1876) and (*Ovens and Murray Advertiser*, 22 June, 1907.)

- Ellen Salisbury building the hut she lived in with Martin Byron. (*Ovens and Murray Advertiser*, 22 June, 1907.)
- Ellen Salisbury's description of hut she lived in with Martin Byron. (*Ovens and Murray Advertiser*, 22 June, 1907.)

Chapter 4

- Joe Byrne hitting one of his sisters in face with a bridle when she allowed a horse to escape. (*The Herald* (Melbourne), 30th June, 1880.)
- Aaron Sherritt having his own selection. (*Ovens and Murray Advertiser*, 29 January, 1874.)
- Aaron Sherritt's relationship with Kate Byrne. (*Ovens and Murray Advertiser*, 29 July, 1879.)
- Evan's Hotel's location in the township of the Woolshed. (*Ovens and Murray Advertiser*, 31 December, 1868.)
- The Vine Hotel's location along Sydney Road. (*Ovens and Murray Advertiser*, 16 May, 1867.)
- Joe Byrne's grandfather a rebel from County Carlow in Ireland.

(https://convictrecords.com.au/convicts/byrne/joseph/130327)

- Maggie working as domestic servant at Vandenburg's Vine Hotel. (Ian Jones, *The Fatal Friendship*, p.176.)

Chapter 5

- Joe Byrne often with the Sherritts. (*Ovens and Murray Advertiser*, 1 June, 1876) and (*The Herald* (Melbourne), 26 July, 1879) and (*Ovens and Murray Advertiser*, 3 March, 1877.)

Chapter 6

- Aaron Sherritt taking a dray load of hay into Beechworth and later being arrested for the poor condition of the lead horse. (*Ovens and Murray Advertiser*, 13 January, 1877.)

- Constable McHugh arresting Joe Byrne in 1875 for stealing John Phelan's saddle. (*Ovens and Murray*, 11 December, 1875.)
- Constable McHugh arresting Joe Byrne in 1876 for the butchering of the El Dorado School cow. (*Ovens and Murray Advertiser*, 1 June, 1876.)
- The location of George Dennett's livery stables. (*Ovens and Murray Advertiser*, 22 October, 1870.)

Chapter 7

- The verdict for Aaron and John Sherritt's cruelty to a horse. (*Ovens and Murray Advertiser*, 13 January, 1877.)
- The incident with Ah On at the dam. (*Ovens and Murray Advertiser*, 16 January, 1877) and (*Ovens and Murray Advertiser*, 15 February, 1877) and (*Ovens and Murray Advertiser*, 1 March, 1877) and (*Ovens and Murray Advertiser*, 3 March, 1877.)

Chapter 8

- Joe Byrne being an opium smoker. (*Police telegram.* VPRS 4965/P0000, 354.)
- The 'letter to the editor' regarding 'heaven Chinee.' (*Ovens and Murray Advertiser*, 22 August, 1874) and (*Ovens and Murray Advertiser*, 3 April, 1875) and (*Ovens and Murray Advertiser*, 6 October, 1877.)
- Joe Byrne's relationship with the Chinese of Sebastopol. (*Ovens and Murray Advertiser*, 10 May, 1872) and (*Ovens and Murray Advertiser*, 8 April, 1873) and (*The Leader* (Melbourne), 1 February, 1879.)
- James Chappell being the licensee of the Reidford Hotel in Sebastopol. (*Ovens and Murray Advertiser*, 3 December, 1878.)
- The initial reporting on the wounding of Ah On. (*Ovens and Murray Advertiser*, 16 January, 1877.)

Chapter 9

- Aaron Sherritt bark stripping in El Dorado. (*Ovens and Murray Advertiser*, 15 February, 1877.)
- Joe Byrne being arrested by Mounted-constable Mullane at Sheepstation Creek on the 6th of February. (*Ovens and Murray Advertiser*, 8 February, 1877) and (*Ovens and Murray Advertiser*, 3 March, 1877.)

- Joe Byrne being remanded in Beechworth gaol for a week. (*Ovens and Murray Advertiser*, 8 February, 1877.)
- Aaron Sherritt being arrested by Constable McCraken on the 6th of February. (*Ovens and Murray Advertiser*, 8 February, 1877) and (*Ovens and Murray Advertiser*, 3 March, 1877.)
- Aaron Sherritt being remanded in Beechworth gaol for a week. (*Ovens and Murray Advertiser*, 8 February, 1877.)
- Joe Byrne's and Aaron Sherritt's hearing before the court of Petty Sessions. (*Ovens and Murray Advertiser*, 15 February, 1877.)

Chapter 10

- Bail secured for Joe Byrne and Aaron Sherritt. (*Ovens and Murray Advertiser*, 17th February, 1877.)
- Ah On's lengthy stay in hospital and the seriousness of his injuries. (*Ovens and Murray Advertiser*, 16 January, 1877) and (*Ovens and Murray Advertiser*, 15 February, 1877) and (*Ovens and Murray Advertiser*, 3 March, 1877.)

Chapter 11

- Aaron Sherritt's sleeping habits. (Francis Augustus Hare, *The Last of the Bushrangers*, p.322.)
- Aaron Sherritt's purchase of lollies from Patrick Allen's store. (The Sun (Sydney), 5 September, 1911.)
- Mary Byrne being taught what to say at the trial. (*Ovens and Murray Advertiser*, 3 March, 1877.)
- Joe Byrne and Aaron Sherritt meeting Dan Kelly in the Beechworth lockup. (*Ovens and Murray Advertiser*, 1 March, 1877.)
- The General Sessions trial. (*Ovens and Murray Advertiser*, 1 March, 1877) and (*Ovens and Murray Advertiser*, 3 March, 1877.)
- The location of Ferdinand Heuss Albion Hotel. (*Ovens and Murray Advertiser*, 26 June, 1877.)
- Ned Kelly being with Dan Kelly in Beechworth. (*Ovens and Murray Advertiser*, 1 March, 1877.)
- Ned Kelly working with Harry Power. (*The Benalla Ensign*, 6 May, 1870.)
- Ned Kelly being treated like a 'black snake.' (*Babington letter*: https://www.ironoutlaw.com/babington-letter/)

- Ned Kelly's views on, and dealings with, Senior-constable Hall and Constable Flood. (*The Jerilderie Letter*, held in the State Library of Victoria.)

Chapter 12

- The General Sessions Trial. (*Ovens and Murray Advertiser*, 3 March, 1877.)
- Aaron Sherritt laughing during the evidence of his brother. (*Ovens and Murray Advertiser*, 3 March, 1877.)

Tales from the life of the outlaw
Joe Byrne

Australian Bushranging

Also available...

Joe was a widow's teenage son with dreams of something better than life on a dairy farm.
Ah Nam was a miner with a taste for booze, women, gambling and fighting.
By a twist of fate their paths would cross and Joe's life would never be the same again.

The year is 1876, and Joe Byrne is wrestling with the loyalty he has to his best friend, Aaron Sherritt, and his loyalty to his family. When Aaron comes to him with a proposition to benefit both parties, Joe makes a decision that will lead him to the darkest place he can imagine: Beechworth Gaol.

The Author

Georgina Phelan (née Stones) was born and raised in Tasmania but has recently made the move across the Bass Strait to reside in Victoria. She has a love of history, with the lives of Australian outlaws Joe Byrne and Michael Howe being her main interests in that field.

She attended school in Ulverstone and has since studied journalism through Deakin University, and history at the University of New England. Her natural inquisitiveness and perseverance have paid off in her work on *An Outlaw's Journal*, uncovering many previously forgotten or overlooked aspects of the life of Joe Byrne, particularly in regards to his early life and connections to the Chinese community.

She also researches and writes for her website *Michael Howe: Governor of the Woods* for which she has been interviewed on ABC Radio, invited to present to the Bothwell Historical Society, and featured in Traces magazine and The Hobart magazine.

The Illustrator

Aidan Phelan is the writer and historian for *A Guide to Australian Bushranging*, an online resource that has been bringing Australia's outlaw heritage to a world-wide audience since 2017. His first novel, *Glenrowan*, depicted the events leading to the capture and execution of Ned Kelly and has sold hundreds of copies around the world since its release in 2020.

He has also published *Bushranging Tales: Volume One* (2022), *William Westwood in his own words* (2022) and *Aaron Sherritt: Persona non Grata* (2022). In 2023, he published two children's books which are aimed at introducing young people to the story of Ned Kelly, both of which he wrote and illustrated. He is working on a similar project about the bushranger Matthew Brady.

Aidan has a Bachelor of Arts and a Diploma of Education, and studied writing and editing at what is now known as Melbourne Polytechnic.

The Outlaw

Joseph Byrne was born to Irish parents in Victoria, Australia, around 1856/57. His father died when Joe was just a boy and he soon looked for work around the Woolshed Valley, where he lived. He spent much of his time with the Chinese in Sebastopol and Beechworth, and with his best friend Aaron Sherritt.

In his early twenties, Joe joined Aaron and Ned Kelly in a horse stealing operation, before being implicated in the police murders at Stringybark Creek in 1878, alongside Ned Kelly, Dan Kelly and Steve Hart. Joe was outlawed, eventually gaining a reward for his capture of £2000. He was an accomplice in two bank robberies and after being coerced into murdering Aaron, was killed during a siege at Glenrowan on 26 June 1880. He is buried in Benalla Cemetery.

www.ingramcontent.com/pod-product-compliance
Lightning Source LLC
Chambersburg PA
CBHW030602310726
48979CB00003B/540

* 9 7 8 0 6 4 5 3 7 8 4 4 3 *